Jessie A. Ackermann

The World through a Woman's Eyes

Jessie A. Ackermann

The World through a Woman's Eyes

ISBN/EAN: 9783744755870

Printed in Europe, USA, Canada, Australia, Japan

Cover: Foto ©Andreas Hilbeck / pixelio.de

More available books at **www.hansebooks.com**

Jessie Ackermann

THE WORLD THROUGH A
WOMAN'S EYES ❧ BY JESSIE
A. ACKERMANN ❧❧ INTRO-
DUCTION BY WILLIAM E.
CURTIS❧❧ILLUSTRATED❧❧

CHICAGO
❧ 1896 ❧

.. TO ..

RICHARD HENRY PRATT

Captain of the Tenth Cavalry U. S. A., and Superintendent of the

INDIAN INDUSTRIAL SCHOOL
Carlisle, Pennsylvania

The Projector and Founder of the Greatest
EDUCATIONAL AND INDIVIDUALIZING ENTERPRISE
In the World

And to the Students of that School, this Volume is Dedicated
with the hope that the great possibilities of the Red
Man may become better known and a deeper
interest awakened in the first
natives of our land.

PREFACE.

Happily, the day has passed when it was the fashion for authors to apologize for their printed works. If a book has no reason for being, no number of apologies can make it acceptable ; if it has a right to existence, no apology for it is necessary. it is left to those who may glance through these pages to determine to which class this little volume belongs.

A word of explanation is, however, due to both reader and writer. Most of the papers comprised in this book appeared in the *Ladies' Home Companion* during the year 1895. All were penned under numerous difficulties of time and place, and with no attempt at literary finish. In short, they are simply a series of rambling notes culled from many chapters in a rambling life. Let the sensible reader take it for granted that the author would cheerfully agree with him in changing whatever he ·would alter, and in leaving out whatever he would omit.

No mention is made in these pages of the great island continent of Australia, where the author spent much time. To present anything approaching an adequate picture of this wonderful land a whole volume would be necessary. Such a work the author has now in course of leisurely preparation, and in due season hopes to submit it to the public eye.

Chicago, Ill., January, 1896.

INTRODUCTORY.

This volume illustrates what a woman who wills can do. While we would not like to have our wives and mothers and sisters and daughters always going about the earth, it is a source of genuine satisfaction to have it demonstrated that they can, if they care to do so. It marks an epoch, too, in the science of travel, as well as in the progress of womanhood when a girl like Miss Ackermann encircles the globe, and visits each continent and archipelago and island to learn what other women are doing, and how they are getting on in the succession of labor and leisure, smiles and sadness, coming and going that we call life. It isn't a very big world, although it looks enormous upon the map, and cheerful and thoughtful men and women will find friends and pleasures and opportunities for usefulness everywhere. Nor is there much peril in traveling. More people are knocked down by bicycles and run over by cable and trolley cars in our cities annually than are killed in railway accidents or lost at sea. Nevertheless it takes courage and ability to cut the cords of conventionality and sail away in any direction that is unknown.

One might use large adjectives and long sentences to describe such undertakings as this young American woman has accomplished if she had not told it so well herself. The privilege of writing an introduc-

tion to this volume included permission to say anything I pleased, and therefore I take the liberty,
without her knowledge, to disclose some secrets about
the author that I am sure will add to its interest and
value.

At once after graduation Miss Ackermann entered
the Temperance Mission Work, and was sent to estab-
lish life-saving stations in Alaska. From that field
she came as a delegate to the great National Convention that was held in the Metropolitan Opera House
of New York, in 1888, and was there appointed a
Round-the-World Missionary of the Woman's Christian Temperance Union.

There have been women travelers before, but I
know of none who have made so extended and sys-
tematic a journey, or brought back so valuable and
interesting a fund of information. In the early days
of the Conquest a young Spanish nun came over the
sea, and carried the story of the Blessed Virgin and
the Christ Child to the savage tribes in all the dark
corners of South America. She wore a rosary at
her girdle, and carried a cross in her hand, and left
behind her an aroma of sweetness and light that
was like a benediction.

In her travels, Miss Ackermann wore the white
ribbon of the W. C. T. U., and with simple, gentle
eloquence made the purpose of that organization
known along a trail that measures 200,000 miles.
She held 1,417 meetings, delivered 870 lectures and
made 447 informal addresses. She spoke the gospel
of temperance and purity upon 41 steamers and

vessels of war, and in 182 pulpits ; she visited 1,140 Sunday-schools, 176 day schools and 69 Bands of Hope ; initiated 647 Good Templars, fastened white ribbons upon 8,479 breasts, and she received the pledges of 7,460 men. She wrote 5,949 letters, 420 newspaper articles, 220 letters to home papers, printed 60,000 leaflets and 2,000 manuals, and raised $8,976, which she expended in her work as she journeyed on. This might have been the labor of a lifetime, but Miss Ackermann crowded it into six short years.

Those who have seen the Southern Cross, hanging like a cluster of jewels in the Antarctic heavens, and have celebrated the Fourth of July upon an iceberg, know that the greatest benefit of travel is to teach the blessings of our own country.

There is sunshine and happiness everywhere, but it hasn't been equally distributed, and there is a very truthful little couplet which a Buddhist priest in Japan once quoted to me :

> " Go East or West,
> But Home is best."

The loveliest music I ever heard was " Home, Sweet Home," played by a band upon the bridge of a battleship in the Mediterranean," and the most beautiful sight I ever witnessed was " Old Glory " floating from the topmast of a little steamer fifteen thousand miles from Washington.

WILLIAM ELROY CURTIS.

CONTENTS.

JAVA AND BURMAH.

INDIA.

AFRICA.

ORIENTAL OBSEQUIES.

ILLUSTRATIONS.

15

ALASKA.

CHAPTER I.

SOME REMARKS ON ENGLISH-SPEAKING WOMEN.

THIS chapter, though seemingly irrelevant to the narrative of my wanderings in far-off lands, is penned with a distinct object in view. What this object is will shortly be made apparent to the patient reader.

Woman has always been an object of interest, doubtless because she "dates so far back." In all ages, men have tried to tell, in story and song, the charms, graces and virtues of woman. We can scarcely turn over a page of ancient or modern literature without reading her praises.

Someone has said, "God's last, best and greatest gift to the first man was woman;" and another,

> " The earth was sad, the garden was a wild ;
> And man, the hermit, sighed, till woman smiled."

I have seen somewhere, a word picture of the first man. He paced the garden up and down; walked beside the rippling stream; listened to the music of the wind among the rustling leaves, and the song of the wild bird; but his soul was not satisfied, and to complete Creation was wrought a masterpiece— "God's last, best and greatest gift to the first man."

These are beautiful tributes to "the sex whose presence civilizes man," as Cowper has it; but how few of us realize that such sentiments have significance for about only one-fourth of the women of the world !

English-speaking women are the recipients of more courtesy and greater civility than those of any other race or tongue. We meet a gentleman, and as a mark of respect he bares his head—we expect him to do it. We enter a crowded room or car, and a gentleman at once rises to give us his seat. It is accepted—sometimes without rendered thanks, I am sorry to say,—as a matter of course, a courtesy due our sex. Yet with all this deference shown us, and all manner of attentions bestowed upon us, there are really few contented English-speaking women. We are alway longing to be something we are not ; reaching for things just beyond our grasp ; trying to climb to heights we can never attain. This longing, yearning, climbing, or trying to climb, has led to a great unrest among womankind. The air is electric with it, and in these days it has taken the form of the " New Woman." Next will come the " New Girl"; with these developments the "Old Man" and the " Old Boy " will have a lively chase to keep up with woman in the race of life. The outgrowth of all this " reaching out " seems to be an increasing discontent among women.

I have just completed a second tour of the world. It covered a period of six years, and during this time I traveled the great distance of one hundred and fifty thousand miles. I was a guest in nearly two thousand homes; all kinds of homes, rich and poor, high and low—from the palace, government house and castle to the thatched cot of the sturdy farmer, the canvas or tin tent of the miner, and the bark hut of the lumber camp. I have seen life in all its varied forms, and under every condition, and I have found few really contented women, so few that they could be counted on my fingers.

What is the matter with these women, do you ask ? Everything. Let me illustrate. I go to one house where everything is beautiful and lovely. Surely, I think, this must be a "heaven to go to heaven in." After I have been there a few days I express my appreciation of my surroundings. "What a pleasant home you have!" I say. The good woman is fully conscious that little could be added, either of comfort or adornment, and she replies, "Yes, I can have anything I want for my home ; I sometimes think I never have a chance to express a wish concerning it ; every want is anticipated."

Here she draws a long breath and continues, " But you know it takes more than a house to make a woman happy. I don't suppose you ever heard—no, I don't suppose you have—but my husband—well, all I have to say is, if you know when you are well off, don't ever marry." With this woman I found the house perfect, but the husband a little wrong. I take her advice and go on my way.

The next house in which I am a guest is a small, six-room cottage. The woman seems perfectly happy,

for she has the "loveliest husband!" She thinks
the Lord never created but just one man, and he is
hers. All his virtues are enumerated ; she tells how
he is the "chief pillar and prop in every good enterprise," and proceeds to give me a little advice, which
I do not take. "If there is another man in the world
like my husband, I should say 'Get married to-mor-
row.'" But she, too, heaves a deep sigh, and fairly
wails out "It's an awful thing, though, to be compelled to live in a small house. When I was a girl
we had plenty of room, but here we cannot have even
one guest. We wanted to entertain you, but really
had no place to put you ; it is almost like living in a
hen-coop." Here the husband is almost perfect—just
faults enough to class him as a human being—but the
house ! Oh, the house !

My observations have not been confined to these
abodes. One day I am being entertained in a lovely
home, where I am the guest of a most gifted woman.
Seeing she has large means and special talents, I try
to interest her in some department of Christian work,
but she exclaims, "For goodness sake don't ask me
to do anything outside of my house ! Do you know I
have ten children?" I told the good woman I was
fully aware of this fact, and reminded her of the six
servants. Her reply filled me with thanksgiving that
I have never had six servants to manage. "Yes, but
the servants are worse than the children ; between
them I have no peace of mind or rest of body ! It
takes me half my time to keep the coachman from
fussing with the gardener, and the other half to settle

disputes between the cook and housemaids. Don't ask me to do anything outside of my house !"

I leave this poor soul, burdened with the care of ten children and the direction of six servants, and tarry in the house of a sad-faced woman who has neither "chick nor child" upon which to bestow her tender care. She goes into the yard, looks over the fence, and sees these ten romping, laughing, happy children. In despair she exclaims, "Well, husband, how do you account for it that the neighbors have all the blessings in life, and we have none?" In one house it is too many children, in the other it is no children, and neither of the women is satisfied.

The greatest curiosity in the form of a discontented woman remains yet to be described. She was of the "New Woman" order. Her family consisted of two beautiful children and "a most desirable husband." She was interested in my travels, the work and the world generally. After a short conversation with her, she clasped her hands and exclaimed, "Oh, what a career; how lovely it must be ! Do you know I have always felt I should have had a mission in the world ; this housekeeping is such a tame life !"

Just think of a woman with a husband and two children looking for a mission ! If I had only the husband, I should think I had the biggest mission on earth. I would never look for a greater. A woman with home, husband and children looking for a mission in this world is far beyond my limited powers of comprehension.

I have tried to illustrate from my observations the discontented state of women who enjoy privileges and opportunities unknown to so large a portion of our sex. If every English-speaking woman could leave her country, and go through the lands where woman exists only as a slave, or, at most, as a "necessary evil," I am sure she would return contented with her lot. She would not pray for greater opportunities, but for "much wisdom" to make the best use of those she has.

We of America need not leave our own shores to contrast our happy condition with the position of our less favored sisters. It is only because of the broader range of vision that has come to us in these last years that woman in some parts of our own country has been released from the degradation of slavery, and elevated to the dignity of womanhood. In this enlightened day we are astonished that our higher civilization has not made itself felt in the release of the women of the far North—Alaska—from a slavery which means not only controlling the labor of their hands, but a right to sell or rent their bodies.

CHAPTER II.

T IS only of recent date that Alaska has been open to travelers—that is, that there have been easy facilities for getting there. But the wonders of the country, when once they became known, created a demand for modern means of travel, and now the journey can be taken, as far north as Sitka, the capital, with quite a degree of comfort. The country belonged to Russia until 1867, when it was purchased by the United States, and with true Yankee enterprise was opened up by the Government. It has now become one of the famous resorts of the Northwest.

Some years ago I undertook a journey to this "Wonderland" of the North American continent in the interests of Christian work. It is not my intention to attempt the portrayal of the physical attractions of this marvelous region; the task has been performed by abler pens than mine. I shall only say that if anyone wants to see the master-stroke of creation, in the form of natural beauty, let him go to Alaska. In no other part of the world can be seen combined, as here, the beauty of the Alps, the glaciers of Norway, the cataracts and cascades of the Yosemite, and the towering grandeur of the Rockies.

And yet, alas, in no other part of the world can be found women more degraded than those who live amid these scenes of God's most wonderful handiwork. In some respects their condition is even worse than that of the women in many parts of Asia.

In the Yukon districts women have so awakened to a sense of their own degradation that many an Indian mother to save her daughter from her own wretched condition throws her away in infancy. These helpless innocents are taken to the woods, their mouths filled with grass, and left to die. The girl children who are allowed to live meet with a worse fate than that of being choked to death with grass. Often, while still infants, they are given away to their future husbands ; or, if kept at home until they are ten or twelve years of age, they are sold for a few blankets or merchandise. About this age a girl is supposed to reach womanhood, and is regarded unfit to mingle with the family. She is confined in a dark room, sometimes for a year, but in some sections for only three months, and is seen by no one but her mother. On emerging from this long confinement her lower lip is pierced, and a bone or ivory ornament inserted, very much as Tamil women pierce their ears and draw the lobe down with heavy metals.

While still young the poor creature often undergoes the painful process of tattooing. As in all barbarous countries, this is considered a great adornment. The colors used in Alaska are red, blue and sometimes black ; but the process differs from that of other countries. Instead of pricking it in with a needle, or after the new device of the Japanese, by stamping, the colors are sewn in, usually on the chin, though I have seen it on the cheeks and breast. They also have a fashion of painting their faces with black paint ; this gives them a most hideous look.

In the streets of Juneau—the largest town in the territory—I passed a number of women sitting in a row against the side of a house. Their faces were all painted black. I supposed this was their means of preserving the skin, but was told it was done to make them attractive and beautiful. They were also bedecked with cheap, showy jewelry, made of silve., bone or copper wire. If civilized women wish to be effectually cured of the barbarous custom of wearing jewelry, they should see heathen women bedecked and bespangled with all manner of tawdry decorations, which, after all, is only the same love for display that characterizes so large a number of women of whom we should expect better things. After seeing women with their ears, lips, nose and chin bored, their toes adorned with rings, and their ankles weighed down with small hoops of bells, they would soon rise above the barbarism of boring their ears and wearing jewelry, both of which are a relic of primeval savagery.

These women of Juneau had their ears pierced from the upper part of the outer rim down to the very bottom. There were as many as a half dozen ornaments in each ear. In addition to these a large silver hoop dangled over the mouth, suspended from the pierced nose. The lower lip did not escape, but came

in for a portion of adornment.   Inserted into the
pierced lip, with one end held between the teeth, was
a piece of ivory, silver or bone, which they removed
and offered for sale.

The inhuman cruelties imposed upon them in childhood, and the utter lack of regard on the part of the
men for all that goes to make up pure womanhood,
increases as they grow older, until the oppression becomes almost unbearable.   The estimation in which
they are held by men has been voiced by one of the
chiefs, who said, " Women are made to labor ; one of
them can haul as much as two men can.   They pitch
our tents and mend our clothing."

On the Upper Yukon a man buys his wives just as
a white man buys his cattle.   If he has wood to cut
or haul, or much heavy labor to perform, he increases
the number of wives instead of purchasing beasts of
burden.   They are regarded from the stand-point of
" a good investment," and only such care is bestowed
upon them as will prevent a "depreciation of value,"
or keep them up to the best service, which, of course,
means the heaviest labor.

In times of war, the men captured are usually
killed, but the lives of the women are spared ; they
have a value in the labor market.   They sometimes
fall to the ownership of men who are most unmerciful
in their treatment of them.   A master's power over
them is unlimited ; it is often a dying command that
several slaves shall be killed that he may have some
one to wait on him in the next world.

The most inhuman treatment these women have to

bear is to be cast out of their houses at a time when
they should have the tenderest care, and suffer alone
the most awful agony known to woman. Frequently
both the mother and child die from neglect.

The word "home" is unknown to these people. The
nearest approach to it is "house"; hence, they know
nothing about home life. To my mind the most de-
plorable condition that surrounds them is the lack of
home life. On the home life depends the development
of the people. This important fact is often lost sight
of in our efforts in Christian work. I once took a
poor, wretched drunkard by the hand, and asked her
to sign the pledge. She said, "It is no use, if I must
go back again to where I came from." I asked her
where she lived, and her reply was, "Come and see."
I went with her to the most wretched place I have
ever entered that passed for a home. It was a dark,
chilly night; we reached the room; she struck a
match and lighted a candle that was made fast in the
neck of an old bottle, and by its dim light I could see
the awful surroundings, scarcely fit to stable a horse
in. She sat down on an old wooden box, and the
tears came to her eyes as she said, "Live here for five
years, and you will be a drunkard, too." I realized
the fact that the woman must have better surroundings before she could become better.

If we are ever to lead these people to a higher civilization, the work must begin in improving the home.
Home life would soon elevate the women above a
slavery so degrading that they themselves feel it.

Dr. Sheldon Jackson, in his wonderful work among

these people, has solved the problem. Along the coast, just out of Sitka — the former Russian capital of the territory—is a native village. Here the people are properly housed, and the children attend the mission school, where they are surrounded by home influences, and see much of home life. The girls are instructed in domestic arts, and the boys apply themselves to various industries. Another village has been started in the direction of Indian river. This is to be a settlement for the young people who marry at the school, and it is the intention to keep them away from the village, and thus prevent a return to their former habits.

Around Juneau, in all directions, from five to twenty miles from the city, are numerous gold mines now in operation, said to contain deposits of great and almost untold value. I decided to visit a certain one of these mining towns before I was fully aware of the means of transit involved in the undertaking. The town was situated in the Great Basin, which I soon learned was accessible only by a mountain trail over which it was impossible for a horse to climb. As the only mule at hand was said to have been thirty-eight years old at the time of the purchase of the territory from Russia (the sale including this venerable quadruped), I decided that my reverence for antiquity was so great that rather than call the long-suffering animal into requisition I would make the pilgrimage on foot, which I did.

Our party made an early start ; as soon as the first

An Alaskan Home.

gray of dawn streaked the sky we were really on the
way. The absence of hotels made it necessary to carry
our provisions, even to a suspicious looking jug—containing cold tea. We were laden almost like camels.
The trail led us over the mountains, through a dense
forest, and beyond rushing streams and dashing water-
falls that seemed to sing an anthem of praise to the
Most High as they hurried on to swell the rolling tide
of the dark blue ocean. We sat down on a great rock
to rest, but the grandeur of the surroundings soon
caused us to forget our fatigue, and we continued to
climb, lost to everything but a sense of the vastness
and greatness of the scenery. We finally crossed the
mountain and reached the valley, stopping at native
huts by the way. These houses are made of bark,
sticks, logs and such material as can be gathered and
put together with but little labor. In some houses
the floor is planked, and a bench about three feet high
extends around three sides of the room; on this is
placed the bedding during the day.

In front of the house stands a totem-pole—an immense timber covered with carvings of the faces of
animals, which represent the tribe to which the family belongs. On one pole can be seen the face of a
whale, a raven, a wolf and an eagle; the lowest figure
indicates to what tribe the grandfather of the occupant of the house, on his mother's side, belongs.
The whole forms a genealogical record of the family,
the child taking the totem of the mother. Beside the
division of these people into the tribes, they are sub-
divided into families, each of which has its badge, or

totem. Members of the same tribe may marry, but
not members of the same badge; a whale may not
marry into the whale family, but may marry into that
of the raven.

The first house we entered was a mere pile of logs
with a bark roof; a small opening in the side served
as a door, but the structure was without windows or
chimney. In the roof was a small opening through
which the smoke passed out, and the earth served as
a floor. The house was without apartments, and the
large room answered all the purposes of kitchen, bed-
room and sitting-room. In the middle of the room,
under the opening in the roof, was a small fire, around
which sat the family, and I should say, their cousins,
uncles and aunts, for they live in a very promiscuous
manner, often as many as twenty occupying one
room. Among the rafters hung great numbers of
fish; the curling smoke, as it made its way upward,
helped prepare them for use in winter.

These people subsist chiefly on berries and fresh
fish in summer, and on oil and dried fish in winter.
They were all eating fish and drinking oil. The oil
is made from a small kind of fish, caught in a seine,
and pressed while alive; it is then placed in tin cans
and kept for the winter. Of this oil they had a gen-
erous supply in a large yellow bowl. A good-sized
ladle, carved from yellow cedar, served as a drinking-
vessel. This was dipped into the oil, and passed
from one to another, each drinking freely, as we
would of tea or coffee. The next meal, without the
least variation, calls the family together again; and

this gathering around the smoky fire, sitting on the
cold ground, eating dried fish and drinking oil, constitutes "home life."

In these places adjacent to the mines women are
degraded below the depths of their native surroundings by contact with the mining element. Men
hasten to mining regions from all parts of the world.
They are either single men, or leave their families behind them, which amounts to the same thing; away
from home influence and the presence of women —
which does so much to keep men from degenerat-
ing—they often sink into most immoral lives. These
men, some of them representing the lowest type of our
race, go to the parents of good-looking Indian girls,
and offer to buy them; or, following a shocking custom that prevails among these people, they offer to
rent them for a year or two. As a result of this state
of affairs, when the men are ready to "move on" to
new fields they leave the native women, often with
young families, wholly unprovided for.

A young lady from the United States was a passenger in the same steamer which conveyed me to the
North. She was a bright young creature, traveling
alone. We sat together at the table, and during the
long voyage of a month we had every opportunity of
becoming somewhat acquainted. This led to her telling me the object of her trip to the territory. For a
long time she had been engaged to a gentleman who
was connected with mining operations in Alaska
which took him there for a few months each season.
He was expecting to return South in a short time, and

the young lady thought she would take the trip, see
the country, surprise him, and enjoy the journey
home with him. I went with her to the hotel where
she expected to find him. Imagine her surprise when
we were directed to a small house and told that he
lived there with his family. For some years he had
resided there during the season, and in a few weeks
he was going South to marry this sweet young
woman. Her counsel to him was, "Marry the native
woman, and be man enough to take care of your children."

Words fail to express what the native women of
almost every country suffer at the hands of white men
who go to their shores in search of wealth, or to follow business pursuits. Wherever the white man has
planted his foot, his tracks may be traced in the
greater degradation of the native women.

A Woman of South Alaska.

CHAPTER III.

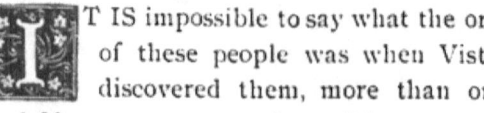T IS impossible to say what the original dress of these people was when Vistus Behring discovered them, more than one hundred and fifty years ago ; so far as I know, an account has never been given. It is but natural to suppose that in the far North their attire was the same then as it is now. The women and men dress alike at the present time, in fur throughout : fur trousers, extending below the knees ; fur-lined boots, with long tops ; a fur jacket, reaching down half way between the waist and knees ; a fur-lined, pointed hood over their heads. Thus they are completely enveloped in fur.

In lower Alaska the manner of dress is very different. In those more accessible parts, where the "ready-made clothing" store has found its way, they have largely adopted our manner of dress— minus shoes, and with the addition of blankets. Some of the blankets are a curiosity. The Chilcat blanket and shirt, woven by the women, often bring a very large price from the money-laden tourists. These are a bright canary color, with the emblems of the country woven in black. The women are most ingenious in their devices for coloring and weaving, the latter being done entirely by hand. The fiber is made from native grasses, dried and twisted till it resembles wool ; this is then woven into shirts and blankets. So slow is the process that many months are required for the weaving of one garment. The dye in which the fiber is dipped is made from the roots of herbs which grow in that country.

Besides the weaving of blankets, the women make hats, mats and baskets. These are straw color, with the emblems of their tribes interwoven in different hues. Large numbers are sold during the tourist season. I have also seen the women at work making silver or bone ornaments, though I am told that most of the silver sold as specimens of Alaskan workmanship is really made in other parts and sent there for sale.

The women participate in all social functions, such as feasts, dances, etc. While in Juneau we learned that there was to be a dance and feast near by which was to last several days ; so we decided to go and see what their idea of dancing was. The people of each country have such different ideas of what constitutes "the dance" that in going from land to land one hardly knows what to expect when it is announced that a dance is going on ; so I started for this with little idea of what it would be like.

The occasion of this "merry-making" was the appointment and recognition of a new chief. The old chief had just died, and the young one, who was to "reign in his stead," must allow the people to do him honor in feast, song and dance. The natives had come from many miles around ; some had traveled days and days to get there. We were in full sympathy with those who had suffered much fatigue in their journey, for we went through dangers and difficulties not a few to reach the scene of festivities.

The spot selected was a bluff, about two miles out of the city, upon which had been erected a wooden house, where the multitudes were to assemble. Toward this we started one night after dark. The path lay along the beach for about a mile ; this led to a very high cliff, the top of which must be reached if we would " go to the dance." It seemed a very difficult task, but by climbing up three steps and slipping back two—floundering about in a most ungraceful fashion—we finally reached the top, and crawled, snake-like, around the ledge, where we sat for a time trying to catch our breath, and congratulating ourselves that we were still alive. It is said, "Those who go to the dance must pay the fiddler," and we had to give our contribution in the form of "climbing to get there."

Foot-sore, breathless, and with blistered hands—to say nothing of rent garments—we reached the dance-hall. The missionary who acted as escort to the party entered first. The master of ceremonies came forward to meet and welcome us. The only available seats were on the floor ; here we arranged ourselves in line against the side of the house where the women were sitting, and soon the uproar began. The most noticeable feature of the gathering was the costume of the women, the chief garment being their Chilcat, or highly-colored blanket. The plain, solid-colored blankets were covered with thousands of white agate buttons. These were sewed to overlap each other, fish-scale fashion, in the most hideous forms, representing the tribe from which they had descended ; or, as we should say, showing " their pedigree "— proclaiming to their small world their " blue blood." Many had their faces painted black, each had rings either in ears or nose, and the crowning ornament— the labret—in the pierced lower lip.

The men wore many kinds of fur. The new chief was arrayed in long bands of white fur, hanging like fringe all around his head, extending down to his chin, and dangling over his face. Less noted ones wore common fur, arranged in similar fashion.

Unlike the custom of most countries the men do all the dancing, and the women look on. The signal was given, and about twenty men stepped to the middle of the floor and formed a circle ; the women sat or piled themselves together around the sides of the room. The " band " was a rattle and a drum ; the latter was hammered without regard to time or tune. Not a foot moved. The dancing consisted in swaying the body, and bending it into every conceivable shape, to the time—if it could be called time —of the music. This lasted until the dancers were ready to drop from exhaustion, when refreshments of oil and fish were passed.

While we looked on in great astonishment some one struck up a tune ; another took it up, then another, until the whole scene became a bedlam of confusion. The women remained seated ; their only part in the dance is to keep time to the music by clapping their hands, and singing a low, sad chant that falls upon the ear like a distant wail of distress. This continues for some days. On the last day they usually "fill up the bowl," and keep on filling up until they fairly reel home to await the death of the chief—looking forward with joy and gladness to a similar occasion.

THE SANDWICH ISLANDS.

CHAPTER I.

A LAND OF MANY CHARMS.

OME time ago I stood on the deck of an out-going steamer, bent on a visit to the Sandwich islands. We waved adieu to our friends on shore and sailed down San Francisco's beautiful bay, nine miles long by fifty miles wide, set with emerald isles, bordered with towns and villages, land-locked by mountains, and dotted with shipping from all parts of the world. A magnificent entrance, one mile wide—Golden Gate—connects this bay with the Pacific Ocean. Through this world-famous gateway floats a commerce second only to that of New York. Sometimes the fog marches in, silent and resistless as an army of ghosts; then again the glory of the setting sun pours through it, lighting up the bay and landscape with a golden radiance. As it was being thus lighted we passed out, with Lime Point on one side, clearly outlined by the pale blue sky, and on the other, high, rugged hills, covered to the summit with green in all shades.

We passed the great rocks over which creep and crawl the ugly, lazy sea-lions, where, protected by the gov-

ernment, they bark and roar, much to the interest of
those who have never seen the " seal-rocks " before.
We crossed the bar, reached the open sea, and before
the shades of night fell were face to face with the
greatest ocean—a wild, weary, trackless waste of water,
stretching five thousand miles away.

As the shadows of departing day lengthened, all
nature seemed imbued with joy ; the very heavens
were tinged with the brightness of another world, and
we imagined we could almost see angelic hands as
they softly shifted the fleecy drapery of the skies.
The sun was lost beyond the horizon ; the pale moon
rose to throw its enchantment over land and sea ; one
great star after another opened its bright eye upon us,
and we were loath to retire to our cabins.

Morning dawned, but the scene was changed. I rose
to make a hasty toilet, but felt compelled to desist, to
retreat—in fact, to retire. The stewardess tried to
comfort me by saying, "It's only a ' swell '; it will
soon be over." The whole day passed, and "the
swell," in fiendish glee, still pursued us. As I lan-
guished in my berth, through the open window came
a voice singing, "Oh, for a life on the ocean wave, a
home on the rolling deep." I could endure the seasickness, but the very thought of those words filled
my whole being with an intense desire to imbrue my
hands in the gore of the man who wrote them to
delude an unsuspecting public. If it were only the
deep that rolled, no one would care ; but the steamer
rolled—everything rolled—I rolled.

As I importuned the stewardess to use her influence

with the captain that the numerous rollings might cease, she mildly replied, " This is nothing ; one time I rolled out of my berth to the floor, under the opposite berth, out into the passage, and should have been rolling still, had I not encountered some deck-hands, who, in the innocence of their profession, mistook me for freight, gathered up my fragments, and deposited me in a place of safety." I spake not another word, for that woman was a better roller than I. I simply resolved that at the end of the journey I should quietly count my bones to see if I were "all there."

I reached my destination in a somewhat weather-beaten condition, but in the first glimpses of dry land soon forgot the discomfort of the sea. It was a charming sight—early in the morning, the air balmy, the bay a beautiful blue, and the sun just peeping above the water's edge, shedding its rays over land and sea. I felt that we had reached a new world.

The first sight of land is Koko Head, a point rising abruptly from the sea, extending into a range of hills, irregular and broken, and covered with many shades of green, making a most beautiful view from the steamer.

The pilot came aboard, and very soon I was landed in one of the most lovely spots that fortune has ever favored me with seeing. Of the eleven islands which compose the Hawaiian group, eight only are inhabited. These include an area of six thousand square miles, and have a climate so charming that hundreds hasten hither as a refuge from storms and blasts.

In Hawaii there are numerous snow-capped mount-

ains, and volcanoes not a few. Mauna Loa is fourteen thousand feet high, and, some years ago, for
twenty days and nights sustained a fountain of fiery
lava seven hundred feet high and from one to three
hundred feet in diameter. It was visible over thirty
leagues away, and by its light fine print was easily
read at a distance of forty miles.

On the side of Mauna Loa is Kilauea, the largest
constantly active volcano in the world. This is
where the ancients worshiped the Goddess Pele ; and
from that crater, at various times, rivers of lava a mile
wide have burned their way through forests and over
villages for thirty miles, and for weeks have poured
their flow of fire into the ocean, killing the fish,
changing the coast-line, and heating the water for
twenty miles along the shore. These mountains lend
beauty to the island, and have a wild kind of fascination for all attracted to the spot ; but the physical
charm of the little republic does not rest in its volcanoes alone. There is a special beauty in the valleys — that quiet beauty of flitting sunlight and
shadow, playing over the smooth surface of softly
flowing streams, that lures one from a world of care
to a calm enjoyment of all that has been created to
turn the thoughts of humanity from the more sordid
things of life.

The most striking feature of the scenery is the
great variety of palms on every hand. The cocoanut
palm is said by Mark Twain to be "the exclamation
point" of tropical scenery. The tree grows very
high—sometimes to the height of seventy-five feet—

Avenue of Royal Palms, Honolulu.

towering up without a branch or leaf until within a few feet of the top, where among the long, graceful leaves can be seen clusters of fruit. This is gathered, at great risk of life, by the native boys, who put the soles of their feet flat against the tree, and, hand over foot, reach the top, a feat to which the whites are wholly unequal. The beauty of the groves is greatly marred by the leaning of the trees, caused by strong sea-winds which blow against them until they incline in every direction and at every angle.

Hawaii is also the home of the banana. Great groves are cultivated by the Chinese. A tree never comes to fructescence but once ; as " the aloe blossoms and dies," so this tree " fruits " and dies, is cut down, and a new tree must take its place, growing from the same roots, before other fruit appears.

One of the chief industries of the island is the growing of sugar-cane. As we drove through the valley great fields of tall, standing cane waved in the breeze, and hundreds of natives were busily engaged in the cultivation of the product that has brought millions to at least one man.

In the lowlands we saw a plant of rare beauty and learned that this was the vegetable upon which the natives chiefly subsist. It has beautiful foliage, with broad, shining leaves very like a calla leaf, and is often grown in our hothouses under the botanical name of *Caladium esculentum.* The root only is used, and is prepared after the manner of mashed potatoes, milk being added until it is reduced to the consistency of cake dough. The natives dip two

fingers into the compound, and thus convey it to their
mouths, never using a spoon. When we visited the
jail it was the time at which the prisoners took their
evening meal, which was served in wash-tubs under
the great trees in the yard. My attention was
directed to a group of natives seated on the ground
around one of these tubs of "poe," all dipping their
fingers in the same tub. It was very amusing to
watch the skill with which the food was taken to the
mouth, without any dripping or stringing about as
one would suppose. This vegetable is said to contain more nourishing properties than those of any
other known plant, and judging from the hearty,
robust appearance of the islanders, I should say it
might be so.

We found nothing of greater interest during the
visit to the islands than the study of the natives.
The present generation seems to be a mixture of all
races. Intermarrying exists here to a greater extent
than in almost any other place of which I know.
The negroes, Portuguese, Japanese, and Chinese
marry white women if they can ; if not, they take
half-castes, and I doubt very much if any of the
present generation have a clear idea of the race to
which they belong.

We passed Emma Hall, and as it was brilliantly
lighted we looked in to see what was going on. In
one room downstairs we found a Portuguese night
school, taught by a half-white teacher. In a room
farther in the rear was a Japanese singing-school,
presided over by a white teacher, an American. In

the hall above the natives were assembled in force,
and an Englishman was trying to lead them into
those paths of sobriety from which they have departed since they were discovered. I doubt if one
roof ever sheltered a more cosmopolitan gathering.

The natives are better housed, clothed and fed than
those of any other part of the world, and are quite as
comfortable as many of the middle class of America.
It is not an uncommon sight to see native families
driving out in their own carriages. Many of the
women are good-looking, tall and graceful of figure,
and are nearly always well dressed. When the missionaries went to the islands in 1820 they found the
women going about in an almost nude state, and introduced what has "evoluted" into the "Mother-
Hubbard" dress. To this the natives have ever
clung, and it forms a most suitable costume for that
clime. They have also made great progress since
their language has been reduced to a written tongue.
Idolatry is now unknown among them ; their idols
are broken, and their superstitions have given way to
enlightenment.

The city of Honolulu has a very large foreign population, and, unlike most cities of its kind, the
natives' houses are found in all directions ; they have
no native settlement or native quarters. They build
pretty houses, own well-kept gardens, live comfortably, and are industrious.

CHAPTER II.

Y VISIT to the islands was in the days of King Kalakaua, who paid me the honor of granting a private audience. I was received in the royal palace, a large stone structure opposite the state-house, situated in the middle of an inclosure containing about eight acres of ground forming a spacious park. This park was inclosed by a fence eight feet high, and each of the large gates was guarded by royal soldiers. It was quite impossible to gain admission to the grounds without an order to the guards. A short distance from the palace, in the same inclosure, was the queen's house, said to be the living-house of their majesties, the palace being used chiefly on state occasions.

Through the courtesy of the chamberlain I was shown over the palace. A long flight of marble stairs led to the great front door, where the chamberlain met me. We stopped in the large hall to see the chief paintings of the palace. They hung on each side of the hall, and were principally those of the dusky-skinned rulers of the past. To the left, through a great archway, we reached the red, or throne room. It was very large, and was furnished in garnet. The chairs were plain, but beautiful— garnet plush with gilt frames. To the far end of the

52

King's Palace, Honolulu.

room, on a small platform under a canopy of magnificent tapestry drapery, stood the throne, plain and
simple, made after the fashion of the chairs.

To the right of the hall we entered the blue, or
reception room, provided with blue brocade furniture
mounted in ebony. On the wall hung the pictures of
the king and queen, and aside from this the furnishings were few and plain. Just before us great folding
doors opened into the state dining-hall. A magnificent sideboard, laden with silver, two long rows of
chairs, a long table, and mixed carpet, completed the
furniture. On the upper floor were the guest-cham-
bers, and those occupied on occasion by the king
and queen. A severe cold prevented the queen from
being present, but his majesty, the king, received me
in the blue room.

This was my first experience in the presence of real
live royalty—a natural-born king—a fellow-creature
great because he could not help it—born great. Poor
man, how sorry I was for him to be thus burdened!
Yet I must nerve myself to gaze upon a sight my
eyes had never beheld. How I felt! My democratic,
Fourth-of-July principles bore down heavily upon me
as I thought of the bowing, scraping and "backing
out" from his natural-born mightiness.

As I sat in the blue room trying to arm myself
with a determination to rise to the occasion, the
shadow of greatness fell upon the floor, and I was in
the presence of this born king. As the chamberlain
presented me the king advanced in a most friendly
way, shook hands, and seated himself near by, ready

to hear any petition I might make. Unlike the
queen, he spoke correct English, and his words were
well chosen. In appearance he was a perfect type of
physical manhood. He was very dark, with black,
curly hair, a feature that at once betrayed the negro
blood. His father and grandfather were both negroes,
but his mother was a South Sea Island woman of
high rank ; so he took his royalty from his mother's
side. He was, I should say, six feet high, weighed
about two hundred pounds, and was both polished
and graceful in manners. He was dressed in a suit
of white pressed flannel, black tie, and canvas shoes.
His display of jewelry was almost alarming; his
hands were covered with jewels of all kinds, each
finger weighted down to the joint, and his spread of
watch-chain was quite overpowering.

While in Siam, I heard a story of Kalakaua that
amused me very much. When he made up his mind
to journey around the world, he decided to visit the
remote and unbeaten regions of Siam. It was announced in the newspapers of that country that this
king would appear amid them in the course of his
wanderings. The Siamese ruler thought it only fitting that his majesty should be received in a most
appropriate fashion, and although well educated in
the English language and quite familiar with the
"lay of the land" of this planet, he could not recall
the Sandwich Islands ; neither could he remember
having heard the musical name of Kalakaua. An
imperial personage, the king's brother, was sum-
moned before the sovereign, and instructed to make

KALAKAUA. LAST
KING OF HAWAII.

EMMA
WIFE.

QUEE
LAST
OF TH
HAWAI

SAMOAN GIRL.

known to him this ruler that was to invade their shores. The prince made all possible speed to gather together his books and begin researches that would lead to information concerning the expected guest. The first book that fell into the hands of the prince chanced to be an early account of Captain Cook's visit to the islands, wherein he read, "The inhabitants are cannibals, or a man-eating tribe." This information imparted to the king, he decided that the hospitality of the palace should be withheld; for he instantly conceived the awful result of a "man-eater" being turned at large among the forty wives, sixty children, and fifteen hundred women in his harem. It is said Kalakaua had to content himself with the accommodations of the hotel.

The king was very unpopular among the whites, and had his days been lengthened, he doubtless would have met the fate of the one who tried to succeed him. The natives, also, were becoming well educated, the spirit of progress had taken possession of them, and they were beginning to feel that the old form of government did not meet the demands of the day, and the rulers were behind in the recognition of the rights of the people.

All around Honolulu are tombs, statues, halls, etc., to perpetuate the memory of past rulers in the minds of the youth. In front of the old native church is the beautiful tomb of King Lunalilo. It is a good-sized structure of modern design, surrounded by a high, iron fence, the gate of which is always locked, so that a near approach to the tomb is impossible. In front

of the state-house stands the statue of the first king,
Kamehameha ("the ugly one"), who subdued the
islands, and set up a kingdom by right of conquest.
The statue stands on a pedestal some five feet high,
and represents the king as conqueror, with a spear in
one hand and the other outstretched and beckoning to
all to come and behold his victory.   He is represented
as very dark-skinned, with no garments save a great
mantle, gilt color, that falls in graceful folds about
his dusky figure.

The mantle of marble gives some idea of the one he
wore during his lifetime.   The original mantle was
made of yellow feathers taken from the breast of a
black bird which was known to the islands in early
days, but which has long since become extinct.   The
king ordered that the birds, which had just one yellow
feather in their breasts, should be trapped, the feather
pulled out, and the birds set at liberty.   From these a
mantle was made said to be worth one million dollars.
It was intended to be handed down to the succeeding
sovereigns so long as a fragment of it remained, or the
islands were under monarchical rule.   The predeces-
sor of Kalakaua became possessed of the idea that as
he entered the unknown he would look well sweeping
through the portals in this kingly robe, so he ordered
that it should form his shroud, and this garment of
vast wealth was consigned, with the king's remains,
to the darkness of the tomb.

CHAPTER III.

N AWFUL and dreaded spot among these islands is Molokai, or leper settlement. The location set aside for the lepers is about three miles long and nearly a mile wide—a perfect place of seclusion. If the poor lepers thought of escaping few of them could do so, for a very high cliff separates them from the other part of the island, so high that clouds most of the time cover its top. To this internment the unhappy victims are doomed for life.

There is no class of people so calculated to draw upon our sympathy as are lepers. The family ties are broken. A father, son, daughter or mother, when declared a leper, is ordered off to Molokai, and no matter what their station may have been, there they must mingle with every and all specimens of humanity, for among the diseased are Japanese, Chinese, half-castes, Hawaiians, and, in fact, members of all the tribes found in the islands. Father Damien, moved by love for the suffering, went to the island to devote his life to the unfortunates living there; indeed, he was banished as were they themselves. Thus he strove for eight years, free from the disease, to administer the comforts of his faith to those who must ever and always, as they look upon their bodies, be reminded that life has few charms for them. Constant contact with the disease brought the good father to see his danger, but too late—he found himself a leper. The signs were faint, but sure. As time passed the disease spread, until his eyes, neck, ears and hands were so bad that it was with difficulty he could perform his usual duties. Father Conrady was sent to the help of this devoted servant of humanity, and doubtless shared the same fate.

At the time of my visit there were some very bad cases on the island, and many were dying daily. From among the fifteen hundred then there, the close of each day found at least one under the sod. Some were without lips and nose ; to some but a portion of their feet remained ; and in others, the disease manifested itself in ways still more repulsive. It was very sad to see small boys, some under ten years of age, with crippled and mangled hands trying to wash and mend their clothes. At the sight of so many deaths these little fellows would say, "If we stay here we shall surely die ; if we could go home we might get well." Little did they dream that they had been sent to Molokai to die.

One would almost expect in the present state of advanced medical science that this disease could be conquered ; but thus far it has baffled all skill. When in the leper settlement off the coast of Africa I met a physician who thought he could arrest the disease if the government would allow him to try. His idea was to inoculate the patient with smallpox virus.

When the news of the many children on the island had spread abroad, and an appeal had been made in their behalf for someone to go there to care for them, Miss Flavin, moved by love that characterizes the women of the world, proceeded to Molokai to devote her life to the young of the leper settlement. On reaching the island, however, it was discovered that she belonged to some different order, and she was thus prevented from carrying out her long-cherished plan of bringing blessing to the lives of the uncared-for of that desolate spot.

South and west of this group of islands the South Seas are dotted with similar groups, varying only a few degrees in climate and tropical scenery. It was my intention to visit these groups on a missionary steamer, and spend a whole season cruising about the Pacific ; but news came to us of swells, squalls and a general disturbed condition of the sea. I had had "swell" enough in getting to Honolulu, so I resolved to continue my journey to New Zealand and later on return to the islands.

On this return trip (to make somewhat of a long digression) we were all delighted to welcome as passengers Mr. Robert Louis Stevenson, the late novelist, and part of his family—his wife and her daughter. The passengers were few, and in the journey of two weeks I saw much of this interesting trio. Mr. Stevenson had been to New Zealand for a breath of cool air in the hope of a general return of strength. From his looks I was of the opinion that his visit had been in vain ; and yet he had no thought of anything

less than entertaining the world for years with his pen,
from which flowed so much that told us of the wonderful genius of the man.   Like his books, he bore
the stamp of genius, and had I not known who he was
I should have said, "There is a man who can say,
'I am part of all I have seen.'"

As I looked at and studied him from time to time
during the voyage, I felt sad indeed to see the physical wreck that was overtaking him.   There is something about the silent fading away of a genius that
makes us feel that others less useful should be the
ones to be borne down the stream.   To see this gifted
man's hollow cheek, sunken eye, and stooped form,
was to see the scythe near his feet, and to know that
time for him was fading into eternity : Robert Louis
Stevenson stood in the shadow of the beyond.

Mrs. Stevenson was also a most striking character,
both in appearance and personality—probably some
years her husband's senior.   From living in the tropics, which means living largely out of doors, she was
tanned, and her skin resembled the color of the Spanish woman.   This, with her white teeth, black eyes
and raven-black hair, gave her a decidedly foreign
look, though she is an American by birth.   Because
of the heat, she and her daughter had adopted the
dress — commonly called a "Mother Hubbard" —
worn by all the Christian natives of the South Seas.
This careless and almost untidy fashion of dress de-
tracted from the dignity of the wife of a genius.   But a
genius—man or woman—has never lived who did not
appropriate unto himself or herself the right of de-

Samoans Preparing Food.

parting from the usual line, either in poor writing or spelling, long or short hair, or some eccentricity of dress, all to help nature out in bearing the stamp of the unusual. These departures, in some form, were plainly to be seen in the three members of this interesting family.

The steamer stopped at Samoa, and I was invited to the Stevenson home, some distance from the coast. Mr. Stevenson had chosen his home there not so much because he favored the spot above all others, but because the gentle breeze from the salt sea — breathed amid the perfume of flowers, under the trees, among all that appealed to his finely strung nature, subdued and softened by the tropical clime—seemed to lend strength to his almost spent forces, and to lengthen the thread apparently so near its end. How fitting, then, that among these people to whom he had endeared himself, and in whose welfare he had so deep an interest—how fitting that he should there have laid down his pen, pushed aside the unfinished manuscript, and asked to be buried on those hills from whose heights he had often listened to the song of the sea beating upon the rock-bound shore, or rolling with soft and gentle murmur upon the sands— that song now changed, alas, into a solemn requiem to the departed Robert Louis Stevenson !

NEW ZEALAND AND TASMANIA.

—

CHAPTER I.

MONG the English dependencies the colonies
of Australasia are the least known, or, if
known at all, are usually associated with
the conditions of primitive days, all marks of which
have disappeared save a few great buildings that stand
unworthy monuments to a system of most inhuman
treatment. When the last of these buildings has
been leveled to the ground little will remain to tell
the tale of early cruelties, and Australasia will be
known to the world as it really is—the workingman's
paradise ; a land of sunshine, fruit and flowers, of
limitless resources and possibilities, and destined to
become one of the greatest republics on the globe.
The remote situation of the islands forming Australasia, the infrequent communication with them, and
the great length of time required for the journey
(five weeks from England, four from Africa, and four
from America), give one the idea that it is a somewhat
unimportant country ; hence extensive travel through
the colonies is a continual surprise.

My first visit was from the direction of the South
Seas ; this brought me to Auckland after a long voy-

age of which the starting point was San Francisco.
The steamers employed in this service are principally
freight boats, and the accommodation is anything but
first-class.   One hundred and fifty names made up
the passenger list ; commercial travelers, tourists and
preachers were among the number.   Every possible
device was resorted to in our attempt to pass the
hours.   As we neared the equator, and the heat became almost unbearable, someone proposed a dance !
The stewards brought out a fiddle and a banjo ; the
passengers formed into line for the Virginia reel, and
"joy was unconfined."   The preachers looked on
and applauded, and one Catholic priest joined in the
dance.   The monotony of the voyage was broken
with preaching on Sundays, and singing, music and
dancing on week nights.   All went well, and we
were having a gay, happy time when we reached the
one hundred and eightieth meridian, where a whole
day was dropped.   Retiring Friday night after the
dance we awoke on Sunday morning.   This brought
two Sabbaths within the six days, which so enraged
the commercial travelers, who had a violent disiike
for that particular day, that they betook themselves
to the smoking-room to play cards.

Among our number were a bride and groom on their
wedding trip around the world.   The bride was a
very young, sweet creature, who had never been
abroad before, and the groom was a bright Englishman, but a wretched sailor.   Poor soul ! it was something pitiful to see him.   I have never known anyone
so affected by the sea.   Again and again he declared

Squatter's Home, New Zealand.

that if he had committed all the sins in the calendar, and broken the entire decalogue, his punishment had far outrun his offense. Finally, when it became unbearable and he could no longer retain a morsel of food after having tried every known remedy, he resolved to abandon the trip and return home. As we neared Auckland he made his intentions known to his bride, who soon rose to a state of revolt, and declared she would go on alone. Auckland was reached, and each prepared to carry out a separate plan, he to return to England by way of America, and she to make her lonely pilgrimage through the distant Red Sea. True to their resolves they each finished their wedding trip alone, and arrived in England in safety.

The approach to Auckland is most beautiful, and reaching it as we did, just when the morning light had bathed the landscape in a sea of glory, we saw it at especial advantage. The long projection known as North Cape extends into the sea at the left, and to the right can be seen a perfectly round island called Rangitoto, which means "the bloody sky." It is supposed that the natives have at some time seen the island in a state of eruption, hence the name. The whole country is of volcanic formation.

Auckland is situated amid a cluster of hills on a small strip of land almost surrounded by water. On the east, an arm of the sea extends inland, almost meeting another arm extending inland from the other side; only a quarter of a mile of land preserves this projection from being an island. The city is quaint

and decidedly English in its life and appearance.
One feature that greatly impressed me was the remarkable degree to which the Sabbath is observed.
The streets are wholly free from traffic of any kind,
and it is only with difficulty that a cab can be hired.
Persons accustomed to driving during the week give
their horses a well-deserved rest on the Sabbath, and
take time to quietly walk to church. Indeed, the absence of rush and hurry forms one of the most refreshing features of residence in this far-away town.
Another thing I remarked was that the common bar-
tender of other lands had here been supplanted by
young women who wholly monopolized the position—
a sight somewhat shocking to those unaccustomed
to it.

About the streets of Auckland I noticed many
swarthy-skinned natives, and was anxious to learn
something of their customs and habits. In appearance they are much like some of the tribes of North
American Indians— tall, well built, with straight
black hair, flat noses, low foreheads, large teeth, and
dark eyes. They speak a language not unlike that of
the Hawaiians, and are very intelligent, more so I
should say than are any of the natives of the South
Seas. When the missionaries first went to New Zealand they found the natives (Maoris) in a semi-barbar-
ous state, given to the worship of idols, and possessed
of the superstitions common to primitive races. Some
of these superstitions they retain to the present day.
The Maoris have been given a section of land known
as the " King's country," where they are comfortably

Shearing-shed. New Zealand

quartered. They are gradually decreasing in numbers, a fact attributed to the introduction of strong
drink, which has a fatal effect upon them. One of
the tribe, a dangerous character, has given the authorities very much trouble. Some years ago, during
the outbreak between the natives and the whites, he
murdered in cold blood forty of the opposing forces,
and although he is a very old man he has caused
much alarm because of his lawless spirit. I visited
him in the Auckland jail, and found a desperate individual who became almost violent in insisting on his
release ; this was finally granted by the authorities on
condition that he go at once to the King's country.
They still have a chief of the tribe who calls himself
king, but he is peace-loving and law-abiding.

Like many natives, these of New Zealand excel
in wood carving. It is remarkable that at an early
day this almost savage race should have displayed
so much skill in this art. In many of the museums
of the colonies can be seen valuable specimens of the
work of present generations.

One of the principal industries carried on by these
natives is the digging for Kawri gum, which is found
in great quantities imbedded in the earth. It is the
gum of the tree which covered the land ages ago.
The supposition is that in some volcanic eruption
these vast forests were buried in the earth, and the
decayed trees left large deposits. The substance is
very hard and flinty, and is largely used in the manufacture of jewelry. When highly polished it resembles amber, and, mounted in elaborate silver settings

makes very handsome ornaments. A green stone, greatly prized by the natives, and often worn by the whites, is also found ; this, too, is polished, and made into charms and jewelry of various kinds.

Leaving the north island, less is seen of the natives, their reservation being wholly in the upper part of New Zealand. I journeyed southward from Auckland in a small boat. This mode of travel always has its penalties attached. It is true the scenery was beautiful — towering mountains, softly murmuring streams, clear bright sky, indescribable sunsets, and views varied by the coloring of blooming fruit trees standing out among highly cultivated lowlands. Under some circumstances I should have gone into raptures over the beauty of nature, but on this little tossing craft, the very movement of which seemed to hypnotize me and place me completely under its spell, I confess the landscape, from my point of view, had very little charm. My only thought was to escape to some place where I could breathe the pure air of heaven free from the combined smell of coffee, boiling soup, curry and all mixtures that can be concocted only on board a steamer. With a sigh of relief I stepped ashore at Napiar, and journeyed overland to the capital, a distance of about one hundred and fifty miles.

Part of the journey was covered by rail, and the remainder by coach, consuming a whole day in crossing the island. About one o'clock in the afternoon our train pulled slowly into the station, where we refreshed the " inner man " and then transferred our-

selves and baggage to the coach in waiting. This
was a time-honored affair—in America we should say
a "forty-niner"—much the worse for wear. Four
decrepit specimens of horse-flesh were harnessed to
this ark on wheels, and soon began to hobble over a
fluted road, every other hobble being an up or down.
Our heads were in constant danger of violent contact
with the "roof" of the vehicle. This ancient conveyance carried a very cosmopolitan company.
Directly opposite me sat a well-dressed, tall and
stately native, or, rather, half-caste ; on one side
was a horse-jockey ; on the left, an Englishman ;
and between these two last, an American. As the
ancient chariot rolled and rocked over the rough
roads, the rattle and clatter of loose windows made
it impossible to hear a word spoken. The Englishman roared something in my left ear, but the rattle
completely drowned his voice. I nodded my head in
assent to his unheard remarks, and our conversation
came to an end. I have a suspicion that I said
"yes" at the wrong time.

In leaving Napiar I had foolishly consented to add
a live dog to my luggage, and see the animal safely
deposited on the other side of the island. Special
provision is made for the transportation of dogs and
the like. A small compartment in the luggage car
affords limited quarters for such "live stock" as may
form part of one's baggage. With oft-repeated protests in the form of prolonged wails and howls, the
dog was jerked into this kennel, and when I left the
train to continue my journey by coach the poor beast

was forgotten. Traveling, as I always have, un-
attended and unattached, it was little wonder that I
completely forgot the live part of my baggage. We
had driven some distance, with such speed as the
disabled horses were able to make, when suddenly
the driver stopped and everyone looked out to see
what had happened. Down the road came two lads
shouting and crying at the top of their voices,
"Driver! driver! the lady forgot her dog." For a
few seconds the driver seemed to speak in a foreign
language—Hebrew, I suppose—and muttering something about women and their cats and dogs he drove
back to the station to recover my forgotten baggage.
All available space inside the coach was taken and
the only place left was the top ; so the poor creature
was dragged to the "upper deck," and the coach
moved on.

The driving was hard, for the road was unkept,
but the surroundings compensated in great measure
for the discomfort. Giant mountains rose on one
side ; and one hundred feet below the road could be
seen the river, winding in and out among the rocks,
its banks fringed with ferns, flowers and creepers that
grew in wild profusion. The striking feature of the
scenery was a native "tree" of the fern family. This
tree is of relatively gigantic proportions, varying in
height from six to ten feet, with long drooping
branches that cluster at the top and shoot out to the
length of six feet. Bird and beast may rest beneath
the cooling shade of the broad and graceful leaves.
In early days the natives used the trunk of these trees

Taking Wool to Station, New Zealand

for building purposes, and some of the buildings thus constructed still stand.

Every turn in the road brought us upon some new scene which led us to forget the shaking of the coach. When the rough part of the journey was over, we were again slowly sweeping the land in an "express" train, which was far from being "up to date," either in matter of speed or equipment. The guard and clerk (conductor and brakeman) were usually lost in the depths of some late novel, or the morning newspaper; consequently passengers were not informed of stops. This necessitated constant watchfulness on the part of the weary traveler lest he should be carried too far and be obliged to walk back. At regular intervals an obliging youth made his appearance to inform us that "meals could be had in the adjoining car." More from curiosity than from the necessity of appeasing a ravenous appetite, I made my way to the dining-car, which was a most primitive affair. The odor of steak and onions and stale boiling coffee bore down upon me as I entered. In the corner, fenced off by an iron grating, stood the cooking apparatus. From the grating, extending lengthwise through the car, was a counter behind which stood a boy ready to dispense "hot steak and onions, chops and tea or coffee." I gave my order and stood—to aid digestion meals were taken standing—while it was being prepared. Having squandered part of my substance on this luxuriant living I returned to the coach, and kept an lookout to avoid being carried past my destination.

Wellington, the capital, is situated on a bay sheltered by surrounding hills, and forms one of the most beautiful harbors of the New Zealand coast. The chief drawback is a strong wind that sweeps the bay at least nine months of the year.

The city is not especially attractive. The principal object of interest is a fine specimen of native carving—a Naon house, a valuable relic of ancient work purchased by the government for the small sum of five hundred dollars. The house was built many years ago as a monument to Camata Waaka Tuarrgere, elder brother of the chief of the natives. It was erected on the Island of Mana, in Poverty Bay, and is of carved totra, a costly native wood. The work was done by some of the most celebrated wood-workers of that day. The building is forty-three feet long, twelve feet wide, and contains thirty-four figures intended to represent the most noted ancestors for many generations past. The work surpasses anything of the kind executed by the present generation, and it was a happy thought on the part of the government to secure and preserve this example of ancient native handiwork. The figures are all about the same size in height, and to the casual observer seem much alike; but when a native enters the room he at once recognizes the figures representing the stock from which his family has descended. The panels are carved on one side only, and are placed, with the most striking effect, at regular intervals of about four feet along the sides of the room. In the same house is a large collection of native gods, the worship of which has long since been abandoned.

CHAPTER II.

HE supreme disadvantage of travel in New Zealand is the necessity for so much of it being done in small steamers. No sooner has the weary pilgrim recovered from the prostrating effects of one voyage than another must be entered on. With a bravery borne of soul-harrowing experiences, and with a resolution worthy of any enterprise, I boarded the steamer for the southern port; and at last, after a repetition of familiar tribulations, we came to anchor in the harbor of Lyttleton, on the east coast of the South Island. The city is built in the crater of an extinct volcano, which surrounds it with high hills known as " The Seven Sleepers." On the summit of each hill, clear-cut against the blue sky, can be traced an outline resembling a person in a recumbent attitude. One of these outlines is so well defined that it bears a striking semblance of the Duke of Wellington, and has been so named. In this neighborhood lies the quiet, sleepy Port of Christ Church, which is passed on the way to Dunedin, the most interesting journey by rail on either island.

As we left the mountains, there was unfolded to our gaze a great fertile valley, extending into the far distance, and beyond it a range of lofty mountains, rugged and seamed by time and the ceaseless action

of the elements. This sheltering range protects the
smiling valley at its foot from the hot and withering
winds of summer, and the blighting chill of winter.
The scene throughout the day was a continuance of
valley-land which bore every aspect of a prosperous,
happy farm life, so softened by the touch of nature
that it brought all things to a complete harmonious
whole. When night overtook us travel came to an
end, for in this country man and engine alike must
rest, which is not a bad plan for those who make
traveling a business. At this point, two hundred
miles still separated me from the spot where the
grand old Pacific rolled in its never-fading majesty
and its never-failing attempt to impress the traveler
with its power.

A whole week of sea was before me. How my
very soul sickened at the thought! How I rejoiced
in the words, "There shall be no more sea." How I
wanted to stand on the beach and declaim to the
waves! I longed to use *large English* at them, and
remind them that the time would come when the last
drop of water would be drained from the fathomless
depths, and even the echo of their song would have
died into unending silence! Just as I was arranging
in my mind a little good, strong English, a sudden
gale sprung up and almost blew us into the bay, and
we sought shelter in the steamer. As if responding
to my mental declamation, the storm broke upon us
in awful fury. The dark, angry clouds hung heavy
on the hills, and as they were reflected in the water
below one could almost imagine the sky lay stretched

View on the Durwent, Tasmania.

upon the earth. The soothing (?) motion of the steamer began before we had cast off from our moorings. If I had signed a contract to "keep my berth down" for a week I would not have done it more faithfully. The most fertile imagination could never conceive the "sensation" in a real storm at sea, unless it had been experienced. The Captain was lashed to the bridge, and never left his post for forty-eight hours. The wind whistled through the rigging with a piping voice, so human-like that it caused a continuous shudder. The heavy tread of the watchman could be heard as he paced up and down, and twice in that night, which seemed to be endless, we heard him call, "All is well!" The stewardess came to tie me into the berth, and inform me that all cooking operations were suspended for the day! The thoughts of a lifetime came trooping before me as I lay in this storm-tossed vessel in mid-ocean, knowing we were simply at the mercy of the winds and the waves.

Two days later we reached in safety the Island of Tasmania. This small island is one of the colonies of Australasia. Although it is only sixteen hours from here to the shores of the main island, for some reason it seems completely shut off from the world. Moreover, it lies under the disadvantage of having been one of the places to which England formerly banished the lawless; and though this element can now scarcely be traced, most of the criminals being dead, yet I can but believe that the influences of the early settlement still have something to do with the lack of progress at the present time in the island.

The climate is perfectly delightful ; for an all-round climate, where one must abide the whole year, I know of none other like it. A strange atmosphere pervades the whole island ; it reminds one of the scripture text, " As it was in the beginning, is now, and shall be for evermore." The home life is charming beyond description. If anyone is seen rushing along the streets, at once a report is circulated that a stranger is in town—for a native Tasmanian was never known to hurry. There is a complete absence of distinguished persons. The only one I have ever heard of hailing from these parts is Mrs. Humphrey Ward, who was born in Hobart. The scenery between Hobart and Launceston is beautiful. It is especially marked by the growth of the fern tree, which is a native of the island, and adds a picturesque effect to the landscape.

Port Arthur is a place of great interest, that is, if one wishes to learn where the prisoners of early days lived and how they were treated. The town is reached in a few hours by boat from Hobart ; the trip gives one a very good idea of the general coast-line, and Port Arthur itself is still attractive. To my mind the object of greatest interest was the old man who had been banished from England for life for stealing some candy from a counter in a bakery to which he had been sent for bread. At the time of my visit he was very old, and had formed such an attachment for the place that he could not be tempted to leave it. He met the steamers when they arrived, and acted as general guide to the visitors.

The old church, which years ago was one of the

A Tasmanian View.

largest on the island, is now in ruins, but the "model prison" was built with such strength that it remains complete to the present day.

This prison was considered the most perfect structure ever erected for such uses, and was, perhaps, the greatest device ever known for inhuman treatment. It so far surpassed anything else that it was regarded as the crowning touch of *latter day civilization.* In grateful recognition of this master-stroke for carrying out the sum of all cruelties, the government pardoned the life-convict in whose fertile brain the plan of this prison originated. The building was made of heavy stone, quarried near by, and was so well built that the years have left no trace upon it. The whipping-post, a heavy iron pillar, still stands; and if it could speak, the very air would, doubtless, become laden with the groans of the suffering. The recreation ground was a small yard surrounded by high walls; to this the prisoners were driven out every day and allowed so many "rounds," twenty rounds making a mile.

When it was necessary to inflict extra punishment the criminal was marched into a dark cell and kept on bread and water served but once a day. I entered this cell, whose very walls might well cry out in protest against the wrongs perpetrated in the name of justice. Four great iron doors, double bolted, barred and locked, shut in the helpless and hopeless victim. Ventilation was not a consideration, for to admit air was to give light, and this vile den was intended to exclude every glimmer of day. The blackness was awful beyond description. Into this chamber of horrors were thrust men and women who in any possible way had rebelled against their conditions.

This direful institution was called the "prison of silence," and was used in punishment of a variety of offenses. Criminals were sent there to be disciplined only, and while within the walls were not allowed to utter a sound; neither were they given any occupation; their lot was to sit in silence for days or weeks. The utterance of a single word meant either the dark room or the whipping-post.

I was surprised when the old convict to whom I have alluded took us to a large room and said, "This is the chapel where they preached to us on Sundays and told us what miserable wretches we were." The room was of circular form, and the pews were fearfully and wonderfully made; they extended around the room from a door on the right to a door on the left, and were so constructed that the "worshipers" could see the preacher only. These pews were in reality only stalls large enough to seat one prisoner; the distance between the rows was about two feet, and the benches were partitioned off at regular intervals with small doors that swung either way. As the prisoner was driven in on Sundays he passed through a number of these doors, and when his own number was reached he took his seat on a bench so elevated that it left his feet dangling in space. The back and sides of each row of seats were so high that the occupant of one stall could not see the occupant of another. Each prisoner was cooped in by himself. In the center of the room the large circular pulpit —

*with soft, pretty drapery, luxurious velvet cushions, and
a beautifully bound Bible* — was filled twice each Sun-
day by a preacher who was paid by the government
to interpret Divine mercy to the unhappy victim of a
cruel and unjust law! Leaving the chapel the prisoners, in profound silence, were marched to their cells
to meditate upon the "Fatherhood of God and the
brotherhood of man," and feel thankful that they
were created to become the means through which a
government preacher could gain an honest livelihood.

An enterprising clergyman has recently purchased
of the government the prison and grounds for a small
sum, and the whole is being converted into a pleasure
resort. It is no longer open as a show place. Most
of the striking prison features are being removed;
and the pews and the pulpit have been taken from the
chapel. I do not know what will be done with these
relics; perhaps they are to be placed in the archives
of the nation that future generations may look on and
better appreciate the progress of their own day.
The chapel has been turned into a billiard-room,
where the walls will resound with the voices of
merry-makers who seek to kill time and care. The
partitions separating the cells will be torn away, and
spacious bedrooms with soft beds and downy pillows
will invite the weary pilgrims to rest in this spot
made *sacred* by the "hand of oppression."

While at Port Arthur I met a government surveyor who had come across the grave of a felon who
was whipped to death. A rough stone marked the
spot, and in rudely chiseled letters we read the fate of

a "prisoner convict." In digging to plant a post near by, a skull was unearthed which was supposed to be that of some one who had suffered a like death. The surveyor had carefully wrapped it up, and was about to send it to the National Museum, but learning that I had an accumulation of curiosities from all parts of the world he kindly donated it to my collection.

It would be a great thing for the prosperity of the island if these buildings, that have made such a sad, pitiful record in human history, could be leveled to the ground, and the last stone cast into the depths of the sea.

JAPAN.

CHAPTER I.

THE MIKADO.—JAPANESE CHARACTERISTICS.

HE world generally is applauding the bravery, courage and pluck of the Japanese. Whole volumes are being written to record their valiant deeds, and the daily press sounds their praises far and near. So, I turn back the pages of my note-book to read my impressions of the race and country derived from personal observation.

The women of Yokohama expected me to reach their shores on a certain day, and appointed a committee to go off to the ship to welcome me and escort me to the capital. We anchored one morning about a mile from the wharf. While engaged in preparation to go ashore I heard someone ask if I were a passenger. Going on deck I found about twenty Japanese ladies waiting to greet me, and see that I landed in safety. They were accompanied by one solitary man, who announced that he had come to welcome me on behalf of his countrymen. The Japanese are so polite, and possessed of such grace of manner that they are frequently called the French of

the East. Special attention is paid to foreign ladies ;
nothing is left undone that can add to their comfort.
This gentleman heard that I had been seasick during
the voyage, so he made me his charge in landing.
As I was about to cross the deck he offered his arm
to conduct me down the steps into the boat. I tow-
ered nearly two feet above him, and as I stooped
down to take his arm my only thought — which
amounted to a fear—was, if I should fall upon this
man he never would know what killed him ; but we
reached the wharf in safety. A hurried drive brought
us to the station, whence in a few minutes we were
whirling northward toward the capital.

The journey was a delightful one, surrounded by
these charming, modest little women, who looked on
me as a born curiosity. The railroad passed through
a beautiful valley ; one side was hemmed in by towering hills, and the other stretched down to the water's
edge. The air was soft and balmy, and the tide was
out, so there was no splash and dash of the waves as
they now and then kissed the sandy beach, rolling
back again to gather force for another caress. The
voice of the sea was scarcely more than a gentle
murmur that came like a soothing lullaby to the
weary traveler.

Traveling is much slower here than in England or
America, and has a decided advantage in giving the
traveler a chance to see as he goes. Thus we journeyed on, skirting the beach until Tokio was reached,
the capital of the empire and the home of the Mikado.

At this particular time, when the eye of the world is on the victorious sons of Japan, who are making history toward which the unnumbered hosts of the future will point with pride, there stands out among the brave, heroic and progressive spirits one of the most striking characters of the century. Unless one has visited the far East, and made one's self familiar by observation with the peculiar surroundings that have from time immemorial hedged in the rulers of these conservative lands, it is hardly possible to understand just what the progressive spirit of the Emperor of Japan means.

When the Mikado came to the throne of his fathers, the one hundred and twenty-first ruler of his line — for he claims an unbroken descent from Jummu Terno, Son of Heaven, who ruled 660 B. C. — he was only sixteen years of age. He had lived the life to which imperial princes for ages have been restricted, and had positively no knowledge of the world, and little foundation for character that must lead, and at the same time rule, forty millions of people. At that time the Mikado was supposed to be the spiritual leader of the people, rather than the ruler, the Shoguns really possessing the temporal power. Some centuries ago the military leaders, styling themselves Tycoons, assumed the power of government, leaving only titular honors to the emperor. The Tycoons ruled with a high hand until Mutso Hito came to the throne, when there was a general demand on the part of his subjects that war be waged with the Tycoons, who had so long kept the real ruler in the background. Therefore it was that in 1868, when only seventeen years of age, out stepped this boy ruler into the nineteenth century sunlight of progress, and brought about the subjection of the Tycoons, who retired into the quietude of private life; and thus the complete restoration of power to the emperor took place.

The spirit of reform was born in the new ruler. In a short time he received the representatives of other countries, being the first emperor who ever sat in state council. Three years later he sent a commission of fifty picked men around the world to study systems of education, and western art and science. He was especially favorable to the education of women. Realizing that much of real character-molding devolves upon the mother, it seemed to him that the better education of woman would aid greatly in laying a sure foundation for the future progress of the nation.

Less than two years after his accession Mutso Hito took unto himself a noble woman to share the duties of his high position. In marriage the emperor is no more allowed to make a love match than is his meanest subject; nor is he allowed to take his wife from any branch of the imperial family; she is chosen from the daughters of the five highest noble families. Imagine this youth, less than twenty years of age, standing before a line of blushing maidens, of whom he has little knowledge, and looking them over much as he might a stock of merchandise from which to select the material for a garment! Knowing nothing of them, he must base his choice largely on good looks. I fancy I see him as his eye runs up and down the line, grasping quickly the features upon which he will decide. And these poor girls! how they must have felt to be inspected from head to foot—to be chosen for looks, or for some feature that might have a special attraction for his majesty! What must their feelings have been as he walked up and down the line, passing one after another till his choice was made, and from the ranks there walked out one envied of all the rest!

Besides the selection of this one woman, who is recognized as the head of his household, and who alone has claim to the title of empress, the emperor may choose eleven concubines. These women are considered perfectly reputable, for they are selected from the best families. Each is established in quarters of her own, consisting of five or six apartments, and has one attendant of certain rank to wait upon her, each attendant having also her servant; thus they form a sort of community to themselves.

The Mikado's choice of an empress proved a very happy one. She was the daughter of a noble of highest birth with a spirit equally progressive as that of the emperor. She is deeply imbued with western ideas, and thoroughly believes in the fullest education of women. She has manifested unbounded interest in the school established for noblemen's daughters, where education in its varied branches is carried on under competent teachers.

During my visit to Japan I spent some time in the school among these charming young women, who are

as eager to adopt western ways as is the empress herself. The one great grief of the imperial household
is that the empress has no children of her own. Ten
children of the concubines have come to untimely
deaths, and two princesses, frail, delicate little creatures, alone remain. At one time, when the emperor
supposed he would be left without an heir to the
throne, he adopted Arisugana Takihite, whom he
intended to succeed him; but when I was in the
country Prince Takihite had been dispossessed, and
Prince Haru had been proclaimed Heir Apparent and
Crown Prince. Since then a law has been passed pro-
hibiting the son of a concubine from inheriting title
or ascending the throne. The heir in future must be
the child of the emperor and empress, or the succession passes to some branch of the family. This, however, will not affect the present prince, who is the son
of the emperor and Madame Yanagewara.

Foreign dress has been adopted at court, and
numerous and amusing are the tales related of the
women who don these garments so "fearfully and
wonderfully made." Accustomed as they are to ease
and comfort in clothing. it was truly a sorry day when
they tried to ape western customs and entered upon
a struggle with our barbarous manner of dress. They
certainly deserve the martyr's crown, and, indeed, I
doubt if that would be adequate compensation for the
torture inflicted by these unaccustomed garments.

When I attended the Tokio dress reform society,
and was asked to express an opinion concerning the
introduction of a new mode of attire, I was in doubt

for a few moments what to say. I looked at them in
their long, loose gowns with roomy sleeves, saw that
they could trip about with a degree of grace, and
certainly with great comfort, and then I thought of
my own manner of dress—of all the stringing, strap-
ping, binding, lacing and hooking! Why it is like
rigging a ship, to get a woman into her clothes in
these days! Especially was it so at the period of my
visit to Japan, for it was the time when woman was
going about (I almost blush to think of it) with a
hump on her back like that of a camel. Since that
fashion has become a thing of the past, I have often
wondered what we would do if we were born with
such a hump; I believe we would lie on our backs all
the days of our lives, trying to flatten it out. I am
often amazed at our lack of intelligence in matters of
dress. We weigh down our poor, tired bodies with
as many pounds of cloth as we can carry, and load
our heads with cockades and feathers until we look
top-heavy and lop-sided; then we go to the mirror,
and the reflection so charms us that we exclaim
"How lovely!" We are then in quite the proper
frame of mind to hasten off to the benighted heathen,
and preach to them of the higher civilization and
what it has done for woman. They listen to our
words, for they are astonished at our appearance, and
simply exclaim, "These poor barbarians! Don't they
know any better?" pitying us from the bottom of
their hearts.

Aware of all this, my only reply to the Tokio dress
reformers was, "Your costume is most comfortable,

and very becoming, and were I a Japanese lady I would always wear it." The women of Asia have suffered much from long established customs, but of one thing, at least, they should ever be grateful to their ancestors — they have handed down from century to century, a style of dress in perfect keeping with the laws of health and altogether modest in design.

In comparing the Chinese with the Japanese the world generally is very apt to overrate the latter. This is especially true at this moment when great victories have been achieved which seem to indicate the superiority of the Japanese over his neighbor. Victory in war, however, is no criterion upon which to base our opinions of the people of these nations. While it is true that Japan has made great progress, and exhibited a spirit of willingness to adopt improved methods of government and throw the country open to the world, it is by no means true that it is in every respect superior to China. Japan excels in warfare ; but that, after all, is only a relic of barbarism, and modern methods of carrying on wholesale murder and butchery surpass in barbarity anything known in the darkest ages. Hence I say, the fact that a nation is victorious in warfare indicates little beyond power for organization. Comparing the two countries from the stand-point of intellect I should say the Chinaman stands first. In morals, it is a case of "drawing straws"; but for logic and philosophy, give me the Chinese.

We of the West, who do not know these people in their home lives, but judge of the whole race by the scattering few who come to our shores, fail to recognize this fact : those who leave China are chiefly coolies—very few of the better class, and none of the high-caste, leave their country. With the Japanese it is just the reverse ; few go abroad to engage in the lower occupations ; and most of those who are found within our borders are either here to attend school or carry on business. Japanese coolies are unknown. As a consequence we are constantly comparing the higher class of Japanese with the coolie Chinese. I have lived in both countries ; I have journeyed away from the beaten tracks of travel, and have had every opportunity of judging the comparative merits of the two peoples. It is true that the Chinaman is slow to grasp an idea ; but when he comes to a decision it is because he has seen the philosophy of it, and from this follows a logical deduction from which it is almost impossible to move him. The Japanese are more emotional, and if their better self is appealed to they move at once ; but when the influence that has affected them is withdrawn they usually slip back to old ways and methods. Because of this characteristic the missionaries do not know just how far to count on them when Christian influence is removed. It is a conceded fact that the Japanese excel in bravery, as the recent war fully illustrates. The Chinese are known to be cowards, and have usually returned from battle with trailing colors. So deeply seated is this element of cowardice that such a thing as a great Chinese general will probably never be known. Perhaps it is just as well, for if ever they become a courageous, warlike people, with their uncounted millions they would soon capture the world.

The Japanese seem never to have drawn the line between time and eternity, and if it were not occasionally so exasperating, it would be really refreshing to move among men and women who take time to live ; but when one goes rushing over the land, anxious to see everything at once, and get away as soon as possible, it is sometimes a great drain on one's reserved fund of grace to possess one's soul in peace and wait for the slow action of the natives.   It is impossible to hurry them ; you might just as well harness a snail, hoping to urge it into a gallop, as to try to impress it upon the Japanese that "time is money."

The country is beautiful, and much of its beauty is due to the fact of which I have just written ; the people take time to cultivate it properly.   It is no uncommon sight to see a man with a wooden plough going over a small tract of land, and another following with grain, planting it in rows with as much care as we would set out cabbage or tomato plants.   On the whole I should say that there is scarcely a race of people who derive more real enjoyment from life than do the Japanese.

CHAPTER II.

HE women of Japan are small—I should say the smallest of the Orient—their average height being only four feet six inches. They are very graceful, have clear skin, and hair—in which they take special pride—as black as a raven's wing. The hair is arranged three times a week, and always requires the assistance of a barber. Even then the process of oiling, gluing and packing the hair into a great pile must tax the time and patience of these women beyond all measure.

I was greatly interested, one day, watching a Japanese lady undergoing this form of martyrdom. She sat on the floor before a small mirror fastened to the top of what we would call a toy bureau. The bureau contained three drawers, in which were kept her articles of toilet—powder, oil, wax and tooth-paste. The barber began operations, and after an hour and a half of hard labor accomplished the feat of massing her hair in a fashion that served as a head-cover, for neither hats nor bonnets are worn ; in fact, the only protection for the head, either from heat or cold, is that which nature has given it.

After the hair of a Japanese woman is arranged it takes little time to complete her toilet. She wears no

under linen whatever, but compensates somewhat for
this seeming disregard of cleanliness by frequent
baths. Her dress is especially to be commended,
both for grace and comfort. It is one garment—a
loose robe that hangs from the shoulders to the feet.
A belt, or scarf, called an obi, is always worn about
the waist, and varies in beauty according to the station of the wearer. It is wrapped two or three times
around the waist, and fastened in the back in the
form of a knapsack, which gives additional width to
the figure, though it cannot be said to add to the
beauty of the costume. The obi is often made of the
richest material, beautifully embroidered, and is the
special pride of the wearer.

The one thing that greatly mars the artistic " make-
up " of a Japanese woman is the foot-gear. Stock-
ings are never worn, but as a substitute a cotton sock
of heavy white cloth, with canvas sole, is donned.
This sock has a slit between the great toe and its
nearest neighbor to admit the strap by which the san-
dal is fastened to the foot. The sandals are of great
variety. The most common are made of plaited
straw—a mere sole piece with a loop that goes over
the foot just below the instep and between the opening in the toe of the sock. Usually, these sandals
are too small for the foot, which hangs over at the
heel. In rainy weather a kind of clog is worn—a
common sole mounted on two pieces of thin wood
about four inches high and six inches apart. This
elevates the wearer four inches, and it is a funny.
sight to see her struggling through the mud in her

Japanese Sleeping Apartment.

narrow dress, with toes turned in trying to keep the clogs on her feet.

The peculiar construction of the houses, and a complete absence of furniture of any kind, make very light housework for the women. In the rural districts the houses are very small, square in form, with thatched roofs. Birds often drop seeds on the housetops, or the wind blows them into the thatching, where they take root, and in the springtime burst into life and beauty. These bright bits of green, peeping out from the roof, lend beauty to the general landscape. The houses are usually built close to the streets, and glimpses of home life are easily caught by the passer-by. In the cities the houses are two stories high ; the lower part is given up to business, and the upper part is set aside for the living rooms. The front—as are sometimes the sides—is made of window-sashes, which slide back and open the whole face of the house to the street. Over the sashes is pasted white rice-paper. The use of window-glass is almost unknown, except among the wealthy, who have copied English architecture. The floors are covered with matting, invariably clean, for neither clog nor shoe is permitted to come in contact with it—they are left outside. The mats are always of a certain size ; a house or piece of land is said to be "so many mats square." These mats are made of raw straw, very skillfully plaited, with a smooth, close upper side. The partitions in the houses are not walls, but sliding screens, which run on grooves, and extend about two-thirds of the distance to the ceiling.

When they are pushed back the whole house is thrown into one large room, which is perfectly destitute of furniture. The floor serves for bed, chairs and table. At night a quilted blanket takes the place of all bedding. The inmates of the house stretch themselves upon the yielding matting, sometimes covered with a clean paper, pull the quilt over them, and place their heads on a wooden pillow, upon which the neck alone rests. Surely, they have little need for a bedstead or mattress.

The leading ladies of the capital entertained me at a native dinner at the Maple Leaf club-house, of Tokio. On reaching the door, I was requested by a servant to remove my shoes, and he at once proceeded to assist me in complying with his request, no one being allowed to enter a house or temple with covered feet. No matter who or what you are, off must come the offending shoes. This done, I ascended a flight of broad steps and reached the great dining-hall, which was without furniture, save the ever-present matting. There was nothing to sit on but the floor. These little creatures drop down on their knees and throw themselves back on their heels—a position to which they have been accustomed from childhood—and the attitude so well becomes them that chairs would be quite out of place. No extra provision had been made for me, and I, too, must sit like a tailor, or squat like a Turk. Being nearly two yards long, I found it no easy task to shut myself up like a jack-knife ; so, camel-like, I got down by degrees and tried to assume as nearly as possible

an attitude like that of my campanions, but even this
kept me so far from the floor, that I was forced to
sit tailor-fashion, in order to reach the food.

Pretty girls came in to wait on us. Before each of
us was set a small tray containing a native soup with
fish dressing. The fish is eaten raw; sometimes, it
is said, while almost alive. This was the first of
about fifteen courses. After an hour and a half had
elapsed, the party broke up. The food that was not
eaten each took from his tray, wrapped a white paper
napkin around it, and slipped it into the corner of
his large, roomy sleeve. This is also a custom in
private houses when " company " dinners are given.

The Japanese are much more liberal in their treatment of their women than are the men of any other
part of the Orient. In most of these countries
women are surrounded by cruel prejudices which,
from the cradle to the grave, compel their submission
at the expense of their greater development and happiness. Although the Japanese women do not enjoy
the privileges secured to their sisters of Christian
lands, their position is greatly superior to that of any
of the women of other parts of the East. They are,
however, without legal status, and their evidence
would not be admitted in a court of justice; hence
they are wholly dependent upon their male relatives
for protection.

Upon the women devolve all the domestic duties of
home life, in addition to which they embroider, clean,
card and weave native cloth. The wives of trades-

men assist their husbands in business, and are said to be very shrewed in "driving a bargain" with foreign customers.

Children are left very much to themselves; there is little mischief they can get into—no chairs to knock about, no tables to overturn. The most they can do is to pitch and tumble about on the soft matting. The older children look after the younger, which relieves the mother of much care. It is a common sight to see very small children at play with babies fastened on their backs, just as the women carry them about while working in the fields. Their playmates are usually a peculiar species of dog, which must be related to the cats of Java, or the Isle of Man, for they, like the cats, have only an excuse for a tail; it is about two inches long.

The only important event in the life of a child before marriage is the ceremony of naming it. On the thirteenth day after its birth the first name is bestowed. If the child is a boy, he receives an additional name when he is married, and another if he ever becomes a government officer; this continues, as he advances in rank, so long as he lives. After death he receives his last name—the one to be carved upon his tombstone—by which his memory is held sacred. The ceremony of naming a child may be witnessed at any time in one of the numerous temples. The child is brought with great pomp and display to the edifice where his parents worship. The process of purification is gone through; then the father hands the priest a piece of paper with three names written upon it.

Each name is copied on a separate piece of paper, and placed in a sacred vessel. They are then shaken up while the priest repeats prayers over them, after which he throws them into the air, and the first piece falling to the floor indicates the name which the gods have decreed shall be bestowed upon the child. The name is then inscribed upon an ornamental piece of paper and given to the father. The priest is required to register the child's name on the temple roll, which is frequently examined by government officials.

CHAPTER III.

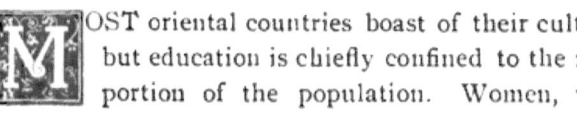OST oriental countries boast of their culture, but education is chiefly confined to the male portion of the population. Women, with but few exceptions—few as compared with the masses—are denied the first rudiments of learning. This is not so true of the women of Japan. Boys and girls alike are sent to primary schools, and since the advent of missionaries special attention has been given to the education of girls, and the higher education of woman is an oft-discussed subject. Many of them aspire to professions, and not a few are engaged in literary pursuits. In Tokio I was "interviewed" by a lady reporter, who was one of the staff of a daily paper conducted by a woman. One of the best temperance magazines of our day is edited and owned by a Japanese woman.

While in Tokio I addressed the "Society for the Higher Education of Woman." The meeting was held in the school established by the government for noblemen's daughters; for the government has awakened to the fact that the advancement of a country depends largely on the development and education of its women. The embassadors to America, England and France are obliged to take their wives with them,

the government having issued the following order:
"Our women are all backward in intelligence for
want of sound education, and the education of the
children goes hand in hand with that of the mothers,
and is an object of highest importance; therefore, we
desire the embassadors to take with them their wives,
daughters and sisters, that they may learn in foreign
lands the correct system of instructing children."

The meeting to which I refer was attended by about
two hundred peeresses. After the address an opportunity was given to ask questions, and it was surprising to see how alive they were to all that pertains to
the advancement of women. They recognized the
fact that the true elevation of the country depended
on their own improvement. No nation can move on
and leave its women behind; it can only progress as
women keep abreast with the age. Several young
girls of rank have been sent by the empress to the
United States that they may have the advantage of
our best schools. Their capacity for advanced mental
training has been fully established by their high
standing in their classes, and the fact that several of
them have carried off first prizes in competition with
American girls of their own age. This will doubtless
lead to placing girls throughout the empire on an
equal footing with boys in educational privileges.
Following this must soon come the legal recognition
of women.

Education in Japan has taken a remarkable form
among some of the better classes of women. The
people are very fond of assembling to listen to pro-

fessional singers and readers. The reading of national legends and romances often attracts hundreds, who listen two or three hours to women who have spent much time and study in preparation for this kind of entertainment. Those who arrive at any degree of eminence have regular places for their performances. I attended one of these, given in a large hall in one of the great cities. We started early, and after getting our tickets, for which we paid fifteen cents each, and taking off and checking our shoes, we entered the hall, took a seat on the clean matting, and awaited developments. Soon the people began to gather—in families, or in twos and threes? Meantime, pretty girls were flitting here and there selling tea and fans, for the evening was very warm.

The hall was hung with the ever-present Japanese lanterns, and the walls were decorated with paintings, many on silk, representing noted persons, or historical scenes. The hall slowly filled. Soon the curtains parted and a woman, in richest attire, appeared before us. Her dress and obi were of the most gorgeous embroidery, but the "construction" of her hair cannot be likened unto anything on the earth or in the sea. It was "wonderfully" built, and adorned with a profusion of hair ornaments, the like of which can only be seen in that country.

She stepped forward, and seated herself on a rug before a low writing-desk, upon which she placed her open book. A most profound silence fell upon the assembly as her clear, well-modulated voice floated out into the hall, reaching the furthermost corner.

Sometimes the reading was accompanied by strains
of low music from an instrument held in her hand ;
then again nothing but the richness of her voice
could be heard. Often, by her gestures or the pathos
of her voice, I imagined a scene of sadness was being
described, or a story of sorrow told. The reading
over, she rose with great dignity and retired, amid
the same silence that was maintained throughout
the whole entertainment.

The education of the women has not yet extended
to the stage ; and such a thing is unheard of in any
country of the Orient save Siam. All parts intended
for women are taken by men in female attire. Among
the common people singers go about the streets in
groups, just as the Italian, with hand-organ and
monkey, wanders through the streets of our more
civilized land. The usual supplications for money
follows the music, and the people are glad to contrib-
ute—I suppose to have them " move on."

CHAPTER IV.

S MIGHT be expected in a land where the will of man is law in the household, divorces are very easy to obtain in Japan. The husband has almost unlimited power. According to the law a man may put aside his wife for any one of seven reasons : First, if she is disobedient to her parents-in-law ; second, if she be barren ; third, if she be lewd or licentious ; fourth, if she be jealous ; fifth, if she have a loathsome or contagious disease ; sixth, if she steal ; seventh, *if she talk too much.* The husband being the sole judge in the matter, these seven reasons could be made to serve in almost any case. The divorced wife has no legal claim to support, but must devise some way to take care of herself. Under no circumstances or plea can a woman get a divorce from her husband.

Polygamy, wherever found, or however modified, is an unmitigated curse. In Japan a man has but one legal wife. She is retained if she presents her husband with the children he desires ; if not, this is sufficient reason for divorce. If he does not divorce her, by common consent, and with her assistance in the selection, he takes one or two " handmaids " into his household, the legal wife retaining her position as head of the house. If she assists in selecting the " handmaid," it is said the wife is never jealous.

A Japanese Lady.

While there are many things in the surroundings of these women which make us feel how vastly better off they are than many others, yet a real searching into social conditions reveals a state of affairs hardly in keeping with their advancement. The sins that abound in other places in the East are found here also. It is true that no painted, lewd women parade the streets and publicly announce their shame ; it is true that no "pestilence walks at noonday" in Japan, but it is there, and a visit to some sections of the great cities makes us realize how the "trail of the serpent" is seen everywhere. Some idea may be gathered from Mr. Humbert's writing of the terrible surroundings into which these women are sometimes led :

"Whither goes that poorly dressed woman, holding by hand a young girl only seven years of age, decked out in her best clothes? After an hour's walk she reaches the external wall of the city of vice, accessible only on the one side—that of the north. She has met no woman on the way. The elegant norimonos of the ladies, whose coolies are carrying them in that direction, are closely shut. Individuals of every rank meet in this part of the city, but salute each other without exchanging the smallest politeness. The houses on both sides of the public way seem to be dependencies of the privileged quarters. The gate-keeper on duty conducts the traveler, with the poor little child, into the presence of his chief. After a few moments the mother and daughter come out of the ward-room, accompanied by a police agent, who leads them to one of the chief buildings in the street. The mother

returns alone, carrying in the sleeve of her dress a
sum of money amounting to about fifty dollars.   The
bargain has been duly made, and has been signed and
sealed.   *She has sold her child, body and soul, for a term
of seventeen years.*

" Majority is only an illusory right in Japan, when
brought in contact with the will of the parent.   In
the greater number of cases these poor creatures are
the victims of the ill conduct of the father, who has
fallen into dissolute habits, and who, in order that he
may be perfectly without restraint, has turned his
wife and children out of his home.   The forsaken
wife will never have an opportunity of contracting
another marriage.   Society condemns her.   If she
has no relations who will receive her, she is left to
utter solitude, and her only prospect is poverty.
Under these circumstances the mother feels forced to
sell her child.   If she be grown up, the bargain is
still better, as the mother will derive from it a small
amount annually for three or four years.

" But what becomes of the girl when the contract
has expired?   She does not retain a farthing of the
money which her wretched profession has brought
her.   She has generally been allowed to go in debt
for dress and food to the proprietor of the establish-
ment, and in order to meet her obligations, she must
enter into a new agreement ; so she generally ends
her life as a servant or housekeeper in the house
where her career began.   If a man happens to form
an attachment for a courtesan, he will purchase her or
even marry her, but such is a very exceptional case.

" The great ladies of these places have their rooms furnished with much elegance. Some of them are under 'the protection' of young men of high families, who pay a certain amount to the keeper, for which she maintains the best looking girls and finest surroundings. Pipes and refreshments are to be had in profusion to season the witty conversation of the ladies as they escort the gentlemen into the garden, surrounded by high walls on all sides. A dance-hall forms part of the appurtenances of the place, and all the dancing is done by the women and the small children, sold at early ages, who figure largely in these performances.

"These resorts are closed to foreigners in Yeddo, but in many localities the government has adopted measures to make these places accessible to the foreign element."

Yet, with all the gnawing away at the very core of home life, one might live in a Japanese city for years and see none of the moral leprosy that nightly flaunts itself in Broadway, the Haymarket, or other streets of the great cities of Christian lands ; but it is there, and the most sorrowful feature of it is the lack of protection to small children who should be in the nursery with their dolls, but who are really the property of parents who barter them in the markets of vice.

CHINA.

CHAPTER I.

FIRST IMPRESSIONS OF THE FLOWERY KINGDOM.

HE country whose name holds fewest allurements for the tourist is China. The lower class of the Chinese have scattered themselves to the ends of the earth, taking with them their vices and unclean mode of life, which have fostered disease to such an extent that the very name of China has become a dread to many communities. It is in this way that the opinions of the outside world concerning the "Flowery Kingdom" have been molded; and because of this, even the most enthusiastic globe trotter turns toward that land with a feeling that is something akin to fear.

As a matter of fact there is far more civilization among the Chinese than we give them credit for. When the inhabitants of the British Isles were painted savages, China enjoyed a degree of cultivation. Wun Wang, who lived during the reign of David, wrote a book that now ranks among the classics, and is one of the standard works in the schools of to-day. When Moses was leading the children of Israel through the

Red Sea, the Chinese were a settled people, having the same form of government under which they now live. Since then the famous empires of Assyria, Babylon, Greece and Rome have waxed and waned, and passed away, and China alone stands the sole relic of patriarchal days.

I confess that the country had very little fascination for me, as I contemplated a somewhat extended trip among the celestials, and I started toward its shores with strange forebodings ; but the day was set on which I was to embark in the "China mail steamer," and there was no drawing back. (Shades of Fulton ! That "mail steamer ! " — a small tea boat with a few cabins in which passengers were to be stowed away for a month !)

I took passage from a northern city on the east coast of Australia, and surmounted difficulties not a few in getting to the anchored steamer, far down the bay. I was taken off in the freight tender—a primitive affair intended only for cargo and live stock. I stood on the wharf while this was being loaded ; saw the sheep and about a dozen Chinese put on, and then I went down with the rest of the live stock. The pitiless rays of a tropical sun beat upon us as, unprotected by awning or cover, we alternately broiled, baked and stewed in that torrid climate. I sat looking first into the faces of the innocent sheep, then at the bland Chinaman —(Oh, the meek and childlike John ! Who on earth can smile like he ?)—wondering which looked the more innocent, when my attention was arrested by a man at one end of the tender

actively engaged in what seemed to be a great labor.
I rose from the candle-box on which I was seated, and
saw he was preparing biscuit. He kept kneading
and kneading away—the perspiration rolling from
his forehead and chin—until his doughy preparation
was ready for the oven, for he was at the head of the
culinary department, and it was near the dinner hour.
Some time later, one of the freight hands, a kind-
hearted soul, asked me if I would have a cup of tea,
to which I assented. He hastened off, and soon returned with an immense, thick cup, brimful of tea,
and beside the cup reposed some of the very biscuit
which the cook had been so recently engaged in man-
ufacturing. I took the tea, and, when the man's back
was turned, fed the fish with the biscuit.

The mail steamer was soon reached, and I found
that I was the only woman passenger booked through
for China. Most of those on board were on their way
to the northern gold fields beyond Port Darwin, of
which place it is said there is only a sheet of brown
paper between it and a very warm climate we sometimes hear of. At this port they all disembarked,
leaving one solitary Jew and myself to continue our
journey.

All went well for a day or two, but the China Sea—
that stormy body of water dreaded by the oldest
and most skillful navigators—fully sustained its repu-
tation, and entered into a conspiracy with the elements
to display their fury. My heart was filled with dis-
may when I heard the captain say, "We are in the
tail end of a typhoon." (If that was the tail end,

deliver me from ever getting into the middle of one!)
The ports were ordered closed, everything movable
taken from the deck, the hatchway battened down,
and all doors bolted. Soon the storm was full upon
us. The little Hebrew was terror-stricken; as for
myself—well, when the captain came to assure us
that there was no danger, I had reached the state
that reconciled Mark Twain to a storm : first he was
seized with an awful dread that he might die, then
with a worse dread that he might not die. I had
reached this last frame of mind, and told the captain
it was a splendid experience from which to gain "dying grace." There is no doubt about it—the sensation of hopelessness that comes upon one in a time
of such awful peril is a good experience.

The tempest lasted three days, and when, at length,
we were informed that we could have our ports
opened, it came to us with a sense of relief such as one
might feel in being resurrected from a too previous
burial. I have seldom had anything so impress me
as the dawn of the day after the storm. The waves,
having spent their force, were content to lie in dark
folds against the ship, tossing it from side to side.
The somber hues of departing night were reflected
upon the bosom of the angry sea, and the gray
of the early morning lent additional weirdness to the
scene. The only noise above the moan of the winds
through the rigging, and the dash of the heavy sea
against the boat, was the steady tramp of the mate
keeping his lonely watch on the bridge.

Three days later, early in the morning, while the

moon was yet high in the heavens, we came in sight
of Hong-Kong. Anxious to catch the first sight of
China I hastened on deck, whence a scene of great
beauty burst upon me. The moon and stars never
shone more brightly—it was almost as light as day—
and we could plainly see on our right the sand-hills
that skirt the mainland, and on our left the larger
hills that form the island on which is built the beautiful city of Victoria. It is but a wee dot in the sea,
consisting of only a range of hills, rising in some
places with great abruptness, and in others gently
sloping to the water. The city extends some three
miles along the shore and up the hills to the summit
of the highest peak, a distance of twenty-four hundred feet. A narrow footpath winds around this hill
to the very top. In addition to this is a recently constructed tramway, a portion of which is so steep that
in looking toward the shore a hair-raising, marrow-
freezing sensation creeps over one.

As we dropped anchor swarms of natives in small
boats descended upon the steamer to take us ashore,
and remained near by till morning was full upon us.
The captain pointed out one of these small boats—
about fifteen feet in length—in which he said, a family
of four generations had been living for years! At
one end of the boat (called a " sampan ") a matting
made of bamboo, extended over a large hoop reaching to the gunwales, afforded protection from the sun.
Under this the entire family ate, slept, cooked and
lived, rarely going ashore.

These scenes around the steamer in the early morning hours, formed a comprehensive and sad commentary on China. The degraded condition of the women is most apparent, and the heavy labor that falls to their portion must make life a burden scarcely to be borne. One woman stood in the end of a boat which was propelled by an oar at the stern, with a child strapped to her back, swaying her body to and fro, trying to quiet the screaming infant and at the same time pulling away at the heavy oar. In one of these small boats I was rowed ashore, where half a dozen Chinamen sprang at me all at once. I was somewhat alarmed, fearing they intended to carry me off bodily; but the captain assured me of their good intention, which was to see that I reached my destination in safety. The choice of conveyance was between a jenrikishaw and a sedan-chair; of these two evils I chose the greater, that is to say, the larger. A chair was placed on the ground, I walked to the end of the poles, backed in, and when seated, a Chinaman in the front, and one in the back, stooped and placed the poles on their shoulders. I was raised some feet from the ground, and thus, high in the air, I was borne through the streets. With a mingled feeling of fear, pity and compassion I passed through the streets amid scenes that no tongue could tell or pen describe. The natives were engaged in every occupation that could be named—from spinning to coffin-making. Not satisfied with the narrow limits of their workshop, which usually serves the purpose of both shop and dwelling, they bring their work to the sidewalk, and ply their various occupations. Thus the whole footpath is taken up, and pedestrians are turned into the road. As the little carriages with their human steeds come spinning along in every direction, the safety of the pedestrian becomes a matter of some concern, and even a stranger will call out to a passer-by, warning him of the danger near.

We passed a stone quarry where women, old and young—some of them very old—were pounding away at the rocks with great sledge-hammers. When broken into small pieces the stones are carried to distant parts of the cities, and used in the construction of new roads. I exclaimed, "How awful!" but the captain told me that such work was not really the most laborious they had to perform. He pointed to the heights of the great hills before us, on which stood many beautiful buildings, and said, "Every stone and stick of timber used in putting up those buildings were carried on the shoulders of the natives, usually the women." In the interior it is a common sight to see a woman and a buffalo harnessed together plowing in the rice fields.

The city of Victoria is decidedly strange in appearance, and were it not for the multitude that throng the streets, it would have the appearance of a ruined town. The buildings are very large, built of brick, and plastered over with concrete. The damp season causes everything to mildew, both in and outside the house. The books, clothing, and everything indoors on which the dampness settles, is covered with minute fungi. Heavy scales of this have accumulated on the outside of the houses, and in the crevices of the stones around the terraces grow every kind of fern and creeper, giving the whole a ruinous aspect which has a peculiar fascination.

Some distance north of Victoria, on the banks of the river which bears its name, is Canton, the largest city of southern China. The teeming millions that hive in this city are truly past all calculation. Indeed, the most astonishing feature of China is the density of its population. If I had been trying to picture the entire population of the earth, I could never have conceived the multitude that here press upon one at every turn. In being borne through the narrow streets of the city, the chatter of the passing throng is almost deafening.

Going down the river the captain pointed out the place where the opium was seized and burned. This caused that cruel war with England in which not only thousands of the people were slain, but which resulted in the greatest evil of the century being thrust upon the populace, for the opium traffic has brought to the venerable empire death in its streets and desolation in its homes. While I was in Canton some Chinese pirates who had looted a coasting boat were captured, and the command had gone forth that they should be beheaded. It would seem that the sum total of all cruelty could be found in the nature of the Chinaman, for his fertility in inventing inhuman means of torture could scarce be equaled this side of the bottomless pit. The Temple of Horrors, within which stand illustrations of different modes of punishment, (some of them not now in practice,) gives

one a small idea of the methods of torture the Chinaman is capable of devising. In bygone days the penalty for certain offenses was to be "sawn asunder."
Long strips of wood, like the staves of a barrel, were
placed around the criminal and made secure by
wooden hoops. Saws were then brought forth and
placed on each shoulder of the victim, and, at a given
signal, the awful work began, and the shrieking
wretch was sawed into three pieces.

Each particular offense had its own punishment.
One was the pulling out of the tongue by the roots.
The savage-looking implement employed in this torture was exhibited in the temple. Another, was to
bring to a white-heat a metal bell, which was placed
over the criminal's head while he was still alive. The
common mode of punishment at present is beheading,
and the execution ground is one of the "sights" of
the city. When the premises are not being used to
dispatch souls into eternity they are converted into
pottery works in which hundreds are employed.

On execution day all work is set aside for certain
hours, after which it is resumed with as little concern
as though the laborers had been away at dinner.
Large earthen jars, piled one upon the other, form
one of the walls of the inclosure. These jars are
filled with the heads of those who have been executed. As the vengeance of the law is meted out to
each criminal the head is deposited in a jar, which is
sealed and given its place in the wall. The bodies
are given to the relatives, if they desire them. The
mode of execution is most primitive. The prisoners

are brought to the grounds chained one to another ;
a heavy stake is driven in the earth, and one of the
victims is led forward with his hands pinioned in
front of him.   He falls upon his knees near the stake,
to which his arms are fastened ; the head is then
thrown forward until the chin rests on the chest,
leaving the back of the neck exposed.   The execu-
tioner steps forward with a sharp meat-ax, and, with
one well-aimed blow, the head is severed from the
body, and is hastily picked up and placed in a jar.

Criminals are usually convicted on circumstantial
evidence, and seldom, if ever, have a proper trial.
Death is not always the penalty meted out to law-
breakers.   For small offenses the criminal is made an
example of.   A large square board with a hole in the
center is placed around the neck and locked with a
padlock.   The criminal is then placed in the public
streets as a warning to those not inclined to regard
the law.   The board is so large that it prevents the
victim's hands from reaching his face, and thus the
poor creature is kept all day from tasting food.   Numbers of these criminals are driven out every morning
and back in the evening, for a greater or less time,
according to the offense.

The missionaries, merchants and commercial men
who live without the wall of Canton form a community of their own.   The life of a missionary is a very
hard one ; so little of the result of his work is ever
seen.   One might pass through the streets of Canton
without becoming aware that a missionary had ever
visited the place.   I heard Dr. Happer, who has just

passed away, and who had been in China forty years, say, "Oh, that I were a young man again! Oh, that I had another life to give to China!" But all those forty years of hard work have left no impress—the city is not even touched by the Gospel; and, humanly speaking, the evangelization of China seems a hopeless task.

CHAPTER II.

O FORM any idea of real Chinese life it is necessary to leave the coast-line and go far from beaten tracks ; this was my intention as I traveled northward.

The absence of rush and hurry in the home life of the Chinaman, and, indeed, in his affairs generally, has its advantage. There has not yet appeared that unmeasured and boundless force, with its very marked strength—that formidable and revolutionary factor in human affairs—the "restlessness" of the masses. In the lapse of ages, and in the course of progressive effort that has laid hold of almost the entire world, China has kept her feet on the rock of her fathers, refusing to enter upon the highway of human welfare hewn out of new ideas and modern thought. The Chinese are not in the least anxious to help make the wide world's history, to see the beginning of new movements, the birth of new ideas, or the development of new theories that will throw open doors that have been closed for centuries. There they stand, four hundred millions strong, as if shut away in the fastnesses of mountain heights, regarding the western ways as barbaric, content to hand down for ages still a civilization that to their minds has served them well. I say it has its advantages, for they are saved the calamity of the mad house, which, in the West, is a woeful attendant upon our civilization, and is beyond a doubt a product of the very culture of which we boast.

The greatest drawback to China is the lack of home life, as we understand the term. Like all the countries of the Orient, the Chinese have no such word as "home" in their language; just what "house" literally expresses, just that thought is their idea of home—a place in which to seek shelter from the storm, to sleep at night, and prepare their food. The greatest need of the Orient is to learn what the word "home" means.

Determined to see something of the home life of these people, I set sail from Swatow, a small place some distance north of Canton, surrounded by a densely populated country. No steamers sail the small rivers, and the only means of travel is either in a small private house-boat, or in one of the public traffic boats that carry the natives from place to place. To travel in the latter entails more or less exposure to disease, for the lower classes have every appearance of deadly maladies lurking about them. Many of them are afflicted with leprosy, making them loathsome to behold. They go about uncared for, and are left to mingle with the masses, thus spreading the disease and endangering the safety of the traveler. Crossing a river in a native boat I have found myself surrounded by lepers in almost every stage of life (or death), yet still able to move about from place to place, veritable walking "pest-houses." When the disease has reached an advanced stage they are awful to behold. The eating away of the various features so disfigures them that they bear little resemblance to a human being.

To avoid contact with these unfortunates I traveled in a small house-boat. This was a novel experience. As we loosed the little boat we were to live in for an uncertain time, and drifted down the bay with the tide, a strange sensation came upon me, and I closed my eyes to mentally peer into the regions beyond, only to feel confused and bewildered as to what we might encounter. The boat had three apartments— the sleeping room, which also served as sitting and dining room ; the kitchen, a small space six by four feet, just large enough for a Chinaman to display his skill in the preparation of food ; and a small room in which the Bible-woman slept on the floor, after the native custom. Besides the cook and Bible-woman, the ship was manned by seven native sailors, who rowed when it was calm weather, and spread the sails when we were favored with a breeze. We were be- calmed much of the time. The weather was hot and damp, for we were in one of those humid climates where everything mildews. A tin box, elevated a few inches from the floor, stands in every room, and in this, on retiring, you deposit the garments worn during the day. If you carelessly leave shoes or books out at night, in the morning they are covered with heavy mildew ; and to hang a garment against the wall necessitates great labor in drying before it can be worn or packed away. After a bath at night, when the vapor almost to the extent of steam rose

from the body, I had serious misgivings as to the condition in which I might be found next morning, and
the "shades" of mould and mildew made wretched
my sleepless hours.

A calm beset us the first night, and taking advantage of the absence of the sun, the men bent to their
oars and toiled all through the hours of darkness.
Daybreak brought us to the mouth of the river, up
which we turned, and encountering the favoring tide,
we drifted with little labor to the sailors. The air
was laden with a salt sea dampness, which caused
every garment to lay hold of the body with a clinging
embrace from which it was impossible to free one's self;
but as it ever is in life, the eternal law of compensation came into full force, and our thoughts were soon
turned to the beauty of the country.

China, in some parts, affords a variety and grandeur of scenery little imagined until the inner regions
are penetrated. Along the Foo Chow river, the traveler finds himself amid the boldest, most striking
mountain scenery through which any known river
sweeps its course ; but the Kitie, the stream up which
our house-boat slowly sailed, wends its curling way
through the lowlands. The banks are dotted with
walled villages, and the whole valley, hemmed in by
distant mountains, is covered with rice and sugar-cane
fields, amid which can be seen the temples, guilds,
and pagodas that form the characteristics of this part
of the world.

The appearance of a foreigner in one of these inland towns is truly an event. So small a per cent of

the people read or know anything of the outside
world that the advent of a white face among them
creates wide-spread interest, and not a little confusion. As our boat came to anchor at one of these
very ancient " villages," where seventy thousand men
and women huddled together within narrow limits
shut in by a wall some twenty feet high, no small
consternation was created. It was noised about that
a foreign boat had anchored without the town.
Crowds gathered, but as night was almost upon us
we thought to remain on board till morning. The
pressing crowd increased in numbers. I looked from
my little window, and saw the banks, as far as vision
could reach, lined with a curious throng, each individual anxious to catch a glimpse of the foreigners ;
for, though they had not as yet seen us, the strange
appearance of the boat plainly told them who its
occupants were.

The Bible-woman thought it would be a good plan
if I would simply step out, let the people see me, and
give them to understand that my feelings were altogether friendly ; for they were beginning to murmur
among themselves, and ask what "foreign devils"
these might be, and for what purpose they had come
to their village. I knew my unusual height (nearly
six feet) would lead them to suppose some giant
race had invaded their borders. What was I to do?
No manner of dress could decrease the two yards
of humanity that would confront them. I put on
my gloves, to avoid contagion from lepers, took
off my sun-bonnet, in which I had traveled, and

Miss Ackermann in Oriental Costume.

with the lady missionary and Bible-woman ventured
into the crowd. When the children saw how I loomed
above the rest they set up a shout, the men chattered
away among themselves, the women came nearer to
examine my wearing apparel, and numerous were the
questions put to us. The missionary who accompanied me could speak the language, and explained
the object of our visit, telling them that we had heard
much of them and their country, and had come to see
what they were like. They seemed quite satisfied,
and we returned to our boats amid many exclama-
tions, such as "How beautiful they are! How
deadly white! Where did they come from?" The
last words the Bible-woman heard were, "That big
one must be a man." The crowd finally disbursed
and we were left to the quietude of the night.

With the break of day, crowds again gathered
about the boat, and when we started for the city it
was with the greatest difficulty that we were able to
reach the narrow streets ; it was impossible to move
in any direction only as we were borne by the crowds.
Their curiosity gave vent to the wildest chatter, and
their strange, unearthly language, and the constant
peering into our faces, occasioned us much discomfort. The Bible-woman, however, assured us again
and again that there was no cause for alarm. Many
of them had never seen a white woman before, and it
was scarcely surprising that we appeared somewhat
strange to them. As we were being pushed and
crowded through one of the narrow streets, on each
side of which, within arm's-reach, were miserable huts

of the lowly, we heard cries and sobs. Stopping in
front of the hut whence the sounds proceeded, we
made bold to enter, and such a scene of human suffering I have never known. On a miserable bed of
straw and rags, in one corner of the room, in a half-
sitting, half-reclining position, was a Chinaman of
that unfortunate class already referred to—the lepers.
He was moaning and sobbing, crying out, "I have
had no rice for two days; I am starving." Hundreds had passed his door, and his cry of distress had
gone forth for more than a day, but no one had
turned aside even to save him from starving. For
five years he had been suffering from the malady, and
his old mother had plowed in the rice fields to support him. She had watched the ravages of the disease, and had seen him grow worse and worse. First
his fingers were eaten away, and there remained
nothing but the stumps of his hands, which he held
out in a most pitiful appeal. Then the lips, the
cheeks, and one ear gave way to the unsatisfied ravages of the plague. The poor mother had looked on
until she could no longer endure the sight of his suf-
ferings; so she concluded it would be far better for
him if he were dead,—and she left him to perish.

Sick at heart from the distressing scene, we made
our way to the great Confucian Temple. The outside of the building bears the appearance of a theater,
with cheap-looking, porcelain finish, which in China
is considered highly artistic. Instead of a spire, or
dome, a collection of hideous nondescript images
forms a central piece on the top of the building, and

the eaves are adorned in similar fashion. The whole
unsightly mass is dedicated to Confucius. The interior is, if possible, even more unattractive than the
outside, though it has been decorated at great expense. The central figure is that of Confucius,
enthroned upon a pedestal under a canopy of heavy
and costly drapery. The image is clothed in rich
apparel, as are also the images of his seventy learned
disciples, ranged around the sides of the room to his
right and left. In front of the shrine an archway is
supported by massive pillars, around which is coiled
a mammoth dragon more than ten feet long. In
China the dragon is an object to be worshiped, and
is viewed with great reverence. It is believed by
the masses that their country, which to them is the
world, rests on the tail of an enormous dragon, who
holds in his power the control of the elements, and
digging in the earth to any depth is strictly forbidden.
Gold has been found on the surface in a number of
places, and it is known that vast coal fields are spread
over large sections; also that beds of valuable and
useful metals lie hidden in the earth. But the peculiar superstitions of the people forbid the development
of these resources. Near the temple great stone tablets have been erected by wealthy admirers of the
prophet who gained for himself a hundred million
followers. Greater and smaller temples to the various faiths are seen in different parts of the city. The
chief characteristic of these edifices is the strange
mingling of rare beauty and great ugliness, of rich
fabrics and inexpressible filth. Chickens wander at

large in these places of worship, and birds and pigeons often roost upon the grinning idols.

The second temple is a plain, square building without ornament of any kind. Around all sides are placed shelves, after the manner of a bookcase, with sliding glass doors. This is an ancestral hall where the records of the dead are placed by their sorrowing relatives. The virtues of the departed are chiseled on small stones, or written on wooden tablets, which vary in size according to the wealth or position of the family, and are placed on the shelves. Before these the mourning relatives pour out their prayers that the soul may go on its way in peace.

When we left this village to continue our journey inland the whole populace turned out to see us off. Some who felt kindly disposed toward us, (those in whose houses we had rested, and where we had spoken to the women,) came down to the boat to bring us presents of eggs and oranges, and taken altogether, I have seldom had a greater "following" than on this occasion.

CHAPTER III.

AFTER some time I returned to Swatow to embark for the far North, but not until I had seen something of one of the customs of the country in which I was deeply interested. I was the guest of a missionary whose husband is at the head of a large hospital in which thousands of women are treated every year. It occurred to me that here was the opportunity to see something of the way in which the feet of the women are made small. I was told that the women had the greatest objection to showing their feet, and my friend, who had worked among them eleven years, had never found a woman who was willing to remove the bandages ; but, nevertheless, we decided to go through the hospital in search of some woman who would accommodate us in this respect, and fortune favored us. We came to one whose feet had been bound for forty years. She expressed a willingness, if taken to an apartment by herself, to remove the bandages. In a small room, seated on the floor, she unwound the strip of cloth that for years had compressed her feet into the smallest possible size, and revealed a horrid sight. It has been supposed by many that the feet of Chinese

women are made to retain their diminutive proportions by encasing them in wooden or iron shoes; but
such means have never been used. The feet are all
made small by binding. A child is taken at an early
age, and a narrow bandage, about an inch and a half
wide and two yards long, is bound about the feet.
One end is placed on the instep and brought over all
the toes but the great toe; this bandage is drawn
with such force that it pulls the toes to the sole of the
foot where they finally grow. Viewing the mutilated
foot from above no toes can be seen, and even when
the sole is examined only the outline can be traced,
for they are pressed in even with the sole of the foot.
The bandages are never removed except to replace
them with clean ones.

I saw a child about ten years old whose parents,
requiring her services about the house, had not bound
her feet until she had reached the age mentioned.
The poor creature could not walk; she was carried
about on the shoulders of natives, and in all probability it would be two years before she could bear her
weight on her feet. The common women, who hew
wood and draw water, or work in the fields, do not
have their feet subjected to this treatment. The binding unfits the feet for any kind of service, hence it
must be confined to the "better classes." I have
seen a full-grown Chinawoman, bedecked in silk and
richest satin, unable to walk across the room without
the aid of a servant or a staff. Her feet were but
three inches long !

It is almost impossible to learn when or how this

custom was introduced; constant inquiry at every reliable source failed to throw light on its origin. In the palace the practice is not carried on. The present ruler, being a descendant of the Tartars, has never allowed this curiously cruel "fashion" to make havoc among the women of his household.

Before leaving Swatow I crossed to the other side of the bay to visit the great Baptist Mission station. We remained longer than we had expected and a night of pitchy blackness overtook us. Our sampan seemed too small to weather a gale should one spring up; so it was decided to send the boatman home, and return in a fisherman's small junk, though even that was considered unsafe. The junk was hailed, and we started across perfectly enveloped in the darkness of the night. It was not more than a fifteen-minute passage to the other side, but instead of rowing, as we supposed the boatman intended to do, he spread his sail when we were part way across, just catching a fierce wind that came sweeping down the bay. This, of course, overturned our craft and threw us into the sea. The Chinese never attempt to save a drowning person; they have some superstition about rescuing people from the water; and for awhile it seemed as though we were destined to perish. Very fortunately, however, a Turkish man-of-war had put into the harbor some time before, and in taking a survey of the bay with its great search-light, saw our overturned junk. The life-boats had been lowered when the vessel anchored; and seeing our distress some Turks sped to the rescue, and we were taken in safety to the

shore. The next morning we sent messages of thanks
to the captain, and a copy of the Bible to each of the
sailors. In over one hundred and fifty thousand miles
of travel this was the only accident that ever befell
me at sea.

We had decided to defer our visit to Shanghai until
the Decennial Conferences, which were to take place
in a short time. A number of missionaries from the
south were also to attend, and for the sake of good
company I decided to wait and travel with them. At
the appointed day about forty, as jolly a crowd as
ever traveled under sail, started northward. They
represented many lands and every shade of religious
belief, but all were bent on having a good time. May
morning dawned bright and beautiful. To keep up
the old-time custom of choosing and crowning a queen
we decided to elect her majesty by popular vote. A
tall gentleman traveling with us, who was somewhat
shocked at the "unconfined joy" of the missionaries,
took it upon himself to maintain the dignity of the
party. To encourage him in his praiseworthy motives,
and show him how much we appreciated his presence,
some of the fun-loving girls proposed that he be the
chosen one. The ballots were passed around and he
was unanimously elected. In mid-ocean there was
little facility for weaving a garland fair for the noble
brow of the male queen, but the ready wit of one of
the young ladies came to the rescue. Scraps of ribbons were clipped from our garments, the crown was
decorated with many colors, and in a fitting speech
the dignified gentleman was proclaimed "Queen" of

the May. All on board participated in the spirit of
the hour, and when night came we were the better
able to sleep for the lively enjoyment of the day.

The steamer was a grand vessel of the French mail
line. From the time it started out from the moonlit
harbor it never gave a lurch, but for two days plowed
nobly through a heavy sea, with the wind blowing a
perfect gale. In good time we anchored at the mouth
of the Whangpoo river, where we were taken aboard
a tender, and two hours later we reached the city.
The change from southern to northern China was
very great. The ever-blooming bowers, rugged hills,
lofty mountains, and trees clothed in perpetual green,
were all left behind as we sailed northward.

From the north of the river to the city of Shanghai
the country is so thickly populated that it gives the
appearance of a continuous city. The river was alive
with all sorts of craft, propelled by oars, canvas or
steam. From the masts, sails and sides of these vessels floated flags and banners, for this was the Chinese
day of days — New Year. It was a pretty sight, as
these gayly bedecked boats passed each other beating
great gongs, waving flags in salutation and wishing
each other good luck for the ensuing year.

The river front of Shanghai, peopled chiefly with
foreigners, has been beautified until nothing more
could be desired in the way of elegant surroundings.
This section of the city has been set aside for the
French, English, Americans and Germans, each forming a community of itself, but all living in most
friendly relations. The city proper is surrounded by

a parapeted wall forty feet high, and is reached
through lofty gateways which at one time could be
entered only at certain hours, and then a countersign
was required. It is one of the greatest cities in
Northern China. On the day of our arrival the
streets were in holiday attire, and the people, arrayed
in their best clothes, gave themselves up to pleasure
and worship. They passed us in swarms, crowding
their way to the chief temple to which place we had
started. In the temple a lively scene was presented,
for many had come to set off fire-crackers, offer sacrifice, or burn incense. There was no special form of
worship; everything was confusion. The people appeared to have no reverence for their "house of worship," but entered smoking, laughing and talking ;
and in the court many different wares were being
offered for sale.

In Shanghai still stands a "baby tower," though it
is no longer in use, the practice of throwing away female children having somewhat died out. In former
times the little girls were often thrown away before the
light of day had fallen on them. It was considered
the only way to avoid the expense of caring for so
worthless a thing as a girl. While it is true that the
baby towers along the coast are no longer used, it is a
fact that there is still little regard for female life, and
the destruction of it is in no way considered a crime.
While I was the guest of a missionary whose house
stood on the river bank, I went into the garden one
morning and saw the forms of two dead children. I
revealed my discovery and was surprised to see what

little concern it created. I was told such sights were very common. The children were, doubtless, unwelcome girls who had been thrown from some of the boat-houses into the river, and the rising tide had left them on the bank; they were probably washed into the stream again to be borne by the onsweeping tide to the open sea. No attempt has been made on the part of the authorities to prevent this wholesale murder of children, and the people are destitute of conscience in the matter, regarding it almost a duty to put an end to the life of girls. I saw a woman who had thrown away seven of her girls, and told of it with the utmost indifference.

A kind-hearted Chinese has opened a Foundlings' Home, to which girls may be brought instead of being thrown away. I paid a visit to this institution for the purpose of seeing what care was bestowed on the castaways. The house stood in a public thoroughfare. I entered a large room, without furniture beyond a row of chairs on each side. Before me was a small shrine canopied by heavy tapestry, and between the parted curtains I saw the image of a woman. In her lap and around her feet were a number of children. The old Chinese greeted me with a polite bow, and in answer to my question informed me that the image represented the Goddess of Kindness. The place was by no means an extensive institution, for it was supported at the sole expense of this humane Chinese. Two nurses cared for seventeen little girls who had been brought there instead of being thrown into the tower or the river.

In bringing children to this home no clue to the
parent is ever given. A small apartment facing the
street is fitted up as a sleeping room for one of the
nurses. In this room a drawer is so arranged that
it can be pulled out towards the street, and in this
drawer is a soft bed for the little stranger. When
the child is placed in the drawer it is pushed into the
room, and in sliding back a spring is pressed which
rings a bell near the head of the nurse, who gathers
in the little waif and it becomes one of the general
household. The children are cared for until they
can walk or talk. If no one comes to adopt them,
a thing rarely done, they are sent to the Buddhist
school to be trained for nuns, many of whom are
found in these parts.

The life of a nun in China is very similar to that of
a nun of the Catholic church. Her life is devoted
wholly to helping those about her. The nuns are in
appearance very unlike the other women of China,
so unlike that they are instantly recognized by their
costume. It is a very unexpected thing to see a class
of women who have adopted a uniform. The costume
of the country has been handed down from all the
centuries. It is a strange fact that four thousand
years ago women walked the streets in the same cut
of dress and with the same peculiar twist of the hair
that characterizes the women of China to-day. But
these devoted women who have set aside their lives
to religious duties, have proclaimed it to the world,
not by long prayers in the market-places but by sober
face and somber garb. The first nun I saw was in

Shanghai. Her long tunic was of a peculiar gray color, more drab than gray ; about her head was twisted some of the same material in the form of a turban ; her hair was closely shaven, and her copper-colored head was partly exposed at the crown. Many of the women who belong to this faith are devoting their lives to the training of castaway girls, most of whom finally become nuns.

CHAPTER IV.

A MISSIONARY CONFERENCE.—AN OPIUM PALACE.

THE great excitement in Shanghai at this time was the coming together of missionaries, from all parts of the empire, who are wont to thus assemble to discuss ways and means and general methods of work. They came five hundred strong, and as some of them were from the very heart of China,—so vast in area, so swarming with human life, so immersed in darkness,—they came breathing the needs of the nation upon the very air that it might be wafted to the lands beyond, and a Macedonian cry fall upon the ears of those in distant countries. Some of these good people had traveled three months, either by cart or mule back, to reach the convention. One missionary walked hundreds of miles, preaching the gospel all the way, and reached the city in an almost dying condition. "But," said he, "I preached a sermon nearly a thousand miles long." The workers of the China Inland Mission came in native dress, which costume they adopt before going into the interior, regarding it as a means of protection. The garments were not unbecoming to some of the sweet-faced girls, but it required a great amount of good looks to offset the rigid severity of the dress.

The men—well, it was positively funny to see them ! When the first one was ushered into my presence it was with great effort that I suppressed a smile. This auburn-tressed son of England had adopted the dress of a better class. The amusing feature of his make-up was a braid of red hair more than a yard long, which hung over a bright red tunic, and by contrast, showed to great advantage. His head was shaven close over the crown, and the small cap afforded no protection from the sun, which had bronzed his face almost to the shade of a Chinese. The loose trousers were bound about the ankles, and his feet were thrust into a pair of cloth shoes with cork soles nearly an inch thick. This was the general appearance of all the missionaries belonging to the Inland Mission.

The conference was full of interest, and only one incident turned our thoughts from the duties of the hour. It had occurred to an enterprising photographer that it would be some time before so good-looking a company would again be found together. This was the moment to give to the world the faces of those who were engaged in the worthy enterprise of spreading the gospel through China. Accordingly he sent his card to the conference with the modest request that they "adjourn to be photographed." The resolution was put to the meeting, the natural vanity of human nature prevailed, and the duties of the hour were deferred for a time. The spot selected for the photographic "ordeal" was a vacant lot where a fine clump of bamboos would form a "background"; and a staging, of amphitheater form, twenty feet high, was erected, with seats from top to bottom. On this staging we were all to arrange ourselves in striking attitudes. Hudson Taylor, of the C. I. M., and his missionaries, in native dress, were seated on the top row ; and others grouped themselves below, friends with friends, and prepared to look their sweetest. While the seating was going on a German missionary made his way towards a young lady to whom he had been paying special attention, and as he carelessly threw himself on the seat upon which her feet were resting, he looked up languishingly into her face and said, " I would so like to sit at the feet of Gamaliel." On a box in front of us stood the artist giving directions for the arrangement of dress and attitude. When we were all grouped into the artistic picture he was anxious to hand down to posterity, he said, " Now, every one look pleasant ; every one smile,"— and behold ! just as our faces were wreathed in our most bewitching smiles, a sudden collapse of the staging brought us all to the ground.

I fell upon the "languishing German," and seeing the blood pour from his nose I asked if he were killed : his reply assured me that he was very much alive. Sandwiched in between several tiers of fellow-sufferers, four or five beneath me, and two or three above, the only movable portion of my body was my head ; this I turned in all directions to grasp the situation. In thus surveying the *fallen mass* I saw one man in a plight at which I heartlessly laughed outright. This same man was noted for his excessive politeness. He had evidently been thrown from a high seat, and the distance had added momentum to his fall; for on reaching the ground he had landed on his back just beyond where I was pinned in by a wriggling mass above and a squirming mass beneath. Two or three men in their hasty descent had fallen over this good brother, and his head was the only portion of his body in sight. Lifting it slightly from the ground he took a calm survey of the scene, and then, with the Chesterfieldian politeness that never for a moment forsook him, he asked, "Gentlemen, may I trouble you to move a little, please?"

The natives rushed into the inclosure from the streets and made frantic attempts to rescue the women. In their efforts to render service they almost disjointed some of us. A Chinaman would take hold of a woman by the arm, and pull away with seven-horse-power to drag her out of the human débris, and as she was thus violently withdrawn it was with sad parting from some of her raiment, making it necessary to beat a hasty retreat. Some of the ladies fainted, and were carried into a house facing the inclosure. In trying to minister to these I lost sight of the rescue work, and when my attention was again directed there, it was to behold an indescribable scene never to be forgotten. All had recovered their footing in a more or less dilapidated condition—hats gone, dresses and coats torn, and umbrellas broken, to say nothing of physical damage sustained. When it was learned that all had escaped death some of the rescued began to sing the doxology. It was then that the photographer should have been on hand to take a

picture, the like of which I never expect to see agai...
This concluded my "down-sittings" and my "up-
risings" with that conference.

In traveling through China it soon becomes apparent that contact with the western world has introduced habits that are anything but elevating to the
people. It is a fact that western civilization without
the subduing effects of Christianity is the worst-
known civilization. It is another fact that the people of the East have fallen into the way of our vices
while our virtues have made no impression on them.
Hence, I should say that they have in no way been
improved by forming treaties with other powers.
These facts are so evident that any ordinary traveler
must be impressed by them, especially if he note how
the people have become demoralized by opium introduced by a western and so-called Christian country.
One of the "sights" of Shanghai is the great opium
palace where the Chinese are debauched by thousands.

In company with several others I made the rounds
of the principal opium "joints," that is to say the
largest places, for a visit to more than a small number
of them would be quite impossible in one evening —
the dens of this one city alone numbering two thousand. The first place we visited was a large structure
three stories high, the whole of which was given up
to opium smoking, as many as two thousand indulg-
ing every night. We reached the "palace" about
midnight, when the greatest number were coming
and going, and the place was fairly teeming with

smokers. The crowds passed us up and down, pushing us to right and left, making it anything but an
easy task to reach the upper part of the building.
The first floor was one large room divided into stalls.
The partitions extended but part way to the ceiling,
and archways served as doors. In each stall was
room for eight smokers. The only furnishings of
these small apartments were divans along the side;
these were three feet from the floor, and about four
feet wide. The smokers were in a reclining position
facing each other, and between every couple burned a
lamp, over which the opium was cooked. Here we
saw men in all degrees of intoxication. Some were
taking their first pipe, paying special attention to the
business in hand; others had taken just enough to
make them happy or silly. One would look up with
an idiotic grin, muttering something in an undertone,
and puffing away at his pipe; another would lie in a
stupor, wholly unconscious of what was going on,
from which he would awake after a time and call for
more opium. The air was black and heavy with
smoke and the fumes of the drug. As we went from
stall to stall we were obliged to fan away the clouds
of smoke before we could see what was going on. On
each floor the rich and poor, the high and low,
through the fascination for this drug, met on the
same footing.

After having visited the dens a few times it was an
easy matter to tell who smoked and who did not, so
decided are the traces of this drug on all who indulge.
Some of the poor wretches seemed to be on the verge

of the grave, they were so wasted in form. Their skin was drawn over their bones and their sunken eyes and strange color told only too plainly of the grim monster that was on their track. In several stalls (though I was told it was not a common sight), I saw mothers smoking, with their babes propped up at their sides, and I have seen little children not more than three or four years of age quite stupid from the effects of the drug. The habit fastens itself upon the helpless victim and he is powerless under it. In one wretched hovel we entered, a dying man was calling for his pipe, which he had not had for a day or two, and his pleading was something awful to hear. At last the medical missionary who was attending him said, "He cannot live anyway, and if it will comfort him any in his last hour, let him have it." It is estimated that there are two hundred millions of smokers in China.

Leaving the ports of China and going inland the mode of travel becomes more difficult. Horses and mules are not common. In many places there are no roads, and the use of carts is impossible. The natives have therefore devised a means of locomotion, unknown in other parts, which seems to them to be a very acceptable way for getting about; but I found it much more fatiguing than any of the other means of travel I had tried. The vehicle referred to is a wheelbarrow. It is somewhat different in construction from that in common use among us, but it is propelled in like fashion. The wheel is much larger, and comes up through the center, with room for a

seat on each side. One is intended for the baggage and the other for the traveler. When I first started out in this strange conveyance there were several things about it that I did not quite understand. In the first place the baggage must balance the rider. I did not know this, and began my journey in a somewhat lop-sided condition. I soon found a missionary going in my direction, and I invited her to a seat in my wheelbarrow. With this young woman and my baggage on one side, and myself on the other, we were properly balanced. The coolie put a heavy strap around his shoulders and fastened the ends to the handles of the wheelbarrow, pushing us with all his might. We made very slow progress, and found it a most fatiguing way of travel. Seated on one limb, and with one foot dangling in a rope stirrup, the position soon became very tiring. I suggested to the missionary that perhaps we would walk awhile and rest ourselves. It would have been well had I learned all about this mode of conveyance before I started, as an untold amount of discomfort would have been avoided. In getting off the wheelbarrow the travelers must step to the ground at the same time. I did not know this, and at my suggestion to walk and rest awhile my companion lightly jumped from her seat to the ground, my weight threw the wheelbarrow out of balance, and I was left by the wayside. I rose from the dust, shook myself, and resolved that at the nearest village I would forever abandon the wheelbarrow, and find some other means of transit— or walk the rest of the distance.

SIAM.

CHAPTER I.

MONG the accessible countries of the Orient, Siam is less frequented than any of the lands having a coast-line ; possibly because it lies just to one side of the usual course of travel, and the vessels running to Bangkok are not the most comfortable in the world.   There is no direct communication between Hong-Kong and Siam ; the steamers are cargo and coolie boats, and anyone wishing to make the trip must be prepared to forego many of the comforts and delights of a large "liner," and resign himself to be carried twenty-four hundred miles by sea when the real distance should be nine hundred.

At Hong-Kong I boarded a small steamer at midnight, and was at once shown by a Chinese steward to my cabin.   We sailed out of the smooth waters of the bay into the ever-restless China Sea, through which I had already passed, and of which I still retained most lively recollections.   Because of the on-coming storm I remained in my cabin for three days, seeing no one but the pig-tailed celestial who, in reply to my question as to the whereabouts of the stewardess, blandly informed me that he was "the stewardess." Three days later, when I was able to get on deck, I encountered the captain for the first time, and to my astonishment found that I was the only white passenger; indeed, the captain, four officers and myself were the only white persons on board. The ship was manned by Malays, Javanese and Cingalese, and was "loaded" with thirteen hundred Chinese coolies, who were being taken to Singapore and Bangkok. In this strange company I was to spend thirteen days. The captain was very kind. When he learned that I was a poor sailor he took other quarters for himself, and had his large, airy cabin made ready for me, which added greatly to my comfort.

The class of Chinese who leave their own country are usually the very lowest, and this cargo of human freight was no exception. To add to their general unattractiveness many of them were afflicted with sore eyes and skin diseases. A portion of the ship was curtained off with heavy canvas, and here the coolies were packed in like so many sheep. They slept on deck on a piece of matting and the usual Chinese pillow, which is made either of crockery or wood. During the day their chief occupation was gambling, and their continuous chatter could be heard through the entire night. Gambling and opium-smoking are forbidden on shipboard, yet it was evident that these rules were not enforced on this boat, for both were engaged in, frequently with unhappy results.

One day, toward evening, I sat in the saloon pon-

dering, weak and weary, over a rusty volume of for
gotten lore—for I was wont, on this long trip, to study
up ancient history. While I was thus engaged, I
heard an unusual sound. Stepping to the door to
see what it might mean I encountered the captain,
apparently greatly alarmed, for he was ashy pale.
Before I had time to speak, he took me by the shoulders, turned me about, pushed me into the cabin, and
locked the door. It was all done in a moment, and no
word of explanation was uttered by the greatly excited captain; I was simply locked up, very much as
a little child might be for punishment. Truth to tell,
I was so indignant at the captain for this school-girl-
like treatment that I almost forgot to be afraid of what
next happened. The noise increased. I heard the
captain order out the guns and swords. A great rush
was made to the room next to the one in which I was
incarcerated, and I could hear the general hauling
down of implements of warfare, though with no idea
of the cause. Before my mind passed a truly awful
panorama—for I thought of pirates, who so often frequent that sea, and feared that if I escaped with my
life at all, it would be to wade ankle-deep through
human blood. These thoughts were banished only
to give room to the idea that it might be mutiny, for
I knew there was little love lost between the captain
and his crew. For two hours the awful suspense
lasted. One can live almost a life-time in two hours
such as those. When at last the captain opened the
door, and I learned that the cause of the commotion
was only a riot, and I had been locked up for fear I

would faint away, my indignation knew no bounds.
It seemed that the gamblers fell into a dispute over
the game, and a quarrel ensued, during which one of
the men was picked up and thrown over the rail into
the sea. The vessel was stopped, and an attempt
made to rescue the drowning man, but without success. The captain could not speak a word of Chinese,
and the only way in which he could maintain order
was to bring forth the guns and threaten the coolies
with instant death. Before we reached our destination a second riot occurred, and twenty men were
taken into port prisoners in chains.

Thirteen days—the most wretched and uncomforta-
ble in my life—brought us to the mouth of the river,
where we anchored to await a favoring tide. The
great waves were left behind, and the salt sea-breeze
gave place to a languid air which lulled us into soft
repose, a state easily reached in that country. On
each side the banks were fringed with tropical vegetation, and in the distance we could see the tall cocoa
and betelnut trees lift their plumed heads like a row
of knights. A delightful sail of twenty miles up this
river brought us to the city of Bangkok, the capital of
Siam.

Arrangements had been made that my first view of
the city should be from the top of a great pagoda.
We steamed off in a little launch and made our way
to Wat Sei Kati. Wat designates the inclosure
around a temple; it contains not only the temple, but
pagodas, shrines, pavilions, preaching-houses, and
many "rest-houses" for the priests. These Wats are

most extensive, and sometimes include numbers of
acres. This particular Wat contains one hundred
and fifty acres.

The pagoda for the top of which we had started
was built of red brick, with a base about one thousand feet in circumference. This was irregular in
construction and had many niches in the wall, showing where Time, the fell destroyer, had left his mark.
The storms of a century had washed the mortar from
between some of the bricks: others had been dis-
placed, and in the cavities thus made seeds had been
lodged by birds or the passing wind. The mist, dew
and sunshine had warmed all into life. Creepers,
ferns, and many forms of vegetation so luxuriant in
that country had twined themselves into a confused
jumble, giving the whole base a ruinous appearance.
The entire structure was about three hundred feet
high, capped by a tall spire extending from the top
of a bell-shaped dome.

Up rickety old stairs, through weeds and grasses,
we made our way, ascending a flight of many hundred steps, winding around spiral fashion, until we
reached the dome, which formed a shrine for a small
image of the Buddha. It was evident someone had
just preceded us, for an offering of flowers and burning incense lay before the god. The ceiling of the
dome was covered with heavy mildew, and in the
dampness and darkness scores of bats had sought
refuge.

This lofty point affords a fine view of the city and
its strange surroundings, the like of which is not

seen in any other part of the Orient. The most striking feature is the long river which forms the chief
thoroughfare. Upon this floats almost every kind of
craft that can be thought of, the most conspicuous
being his majesty's war-vessels anchored near the
landing. Tiny skiffs—hardly large enough to hold
a good-sized dog—hewn out of small trees from the
the jungle, float among the curtained, canvased, and
gilded barges of the nobles. All conditions and
classes ply their boats in endless activity, day and
night, over the smooth surface of the water. On the
bosom of this river is carried on all the trade and
traffic of the vast city, equal in size to any in the
world. At a central point, very early in the morning, the natives gather at the water market with their
boats, laden almost to sinking with rice, vegetables
and fish, all of which must be sold before the sun is
high in the heavens. It is a wonderful sight, though
somewhat confusing. Old women, wrinkled and worn
and scantily clad, cry out their wares in sharp and
shrill tones, while small children, both boys and girls,
try to outcry them. The noise and bustle continue
for some hours, when the venders return to their
place of rest for food and a midday nap ; there they
remain until the sun disappears behind the towering
cocoanut and betel trees.

Unlike the Chinese, these people live in boat
houses instead of house-boats. The houses are regu-
larly constructed with apartments and living conven-
iences, and a boat bottom made of rafters. Heavy
posts are driven into the bed of the river, along each

bank, to which the houses are made fast either by
ropes or chains. In going up or down the river it
is a common sight to see a private house or a shop
floating with the tide, looking for a better business
place, or, perhaps, more congenial neighbors. Thus,
thousands and thousands live, floating and drifting
their time and lives away. From the river, in all
directions, are water-courses, used as streets, forming
a perfect network of canals through the entire city.

The foreign population live on the land, but because of these waterways it is necessary to travel in
house-boats. In the center of a small skiff a shelter
is built for protection from the sun, which often
proves fatal to the careless. In this small space
business men are rowed to and from their offices.
Usually, six oarsmen are required, four at the oars
and a relay of two. This mode of travel is most trying to one accustomed to rapid transit; and in getting to and from places much time is lost that might
be otherwise utilized with profit.

CHAPTER II.

THE greater part of the habitations of Bangkok are found upon the river. The dwellings on the land help to make up the variety in that far-away place. The drive on the mainland is known as the King's Road, in which I saw different but not greater sights than those along the river. The street scenes are a moving, ever-changing panorama. As we drove along, there trooped past me women and children of many shades and nationalities. I was told that no less than fifteen nationalities passed us, all dark-skinned. Of these, standing out most conspicuous, was a class of men seen in different attire in all parts of Asia—the ever-present Buddhist priest. In Siam they are more noticeable because of their peculiar dress, which is a very bright yellow. The garment hangs in graceful folds about the body, one shoulder being exposed, while over the other is thrown a long narrow strip of silk the color of the robe.

Hundreds of these priests are seen daily in the streets. The religion of the country requires each man to enter the priesthood for three years of his life, during which time he must withdraw from his family, and live in the temple grounds. The priests are supported by alms from the common people,—and in Bangkok alone, thirty thousand able-bodied men are thus maintained in indolence. They are required to beg their food each day, gathering only a sufficient amount for two meals, which they are supposed to take in the twenty-four hours. Because of the severe heat, all classes bestir themselves while we are still wont to slumber. As soon as the gray dawn streaks the morning sky, the first thing to meet the eye is the begging priest, with his yellow robes flowing in the breeze. With a large brown bowl under his arm, he goes from house to house where the morning meal is being prepared, and begs a spoonful of rice from each cooking-pot. When his bowl is filled, he returns to the temple grounds, where most of the day is spent in reading and prayer.

In my wanderings I came across numbers of them reading from their sacred books, a copy of which I very much desired. I asked my guide to try to buy one, but the devout priest told him he dared not sell it, though if I would put the silver down he would go away while I took the volume. His conscience being thus easily satisfied, I became the possessor of one of these books, which is a great curiosity. The letters are scratched by some sharp-pointed instrument on long polished strips from the fan palm-tree. When these artistic characters have been formed, the leaf is rubbed with a black preparation to bring out the letters. The strips are then placed one upon the other in the order of reading, and the whole is bound together with a silk cord.

Besides the groups of priests hurrying by, could be seen great numbers of Chinese. In this warm climate, if possible more enervating than that of their own country, they have adopted the Siamese fashion of dispensing, practically, with clothing. One of the most embarrassing situations to a stranger is to encounter these people in their scanty apparel—an apology only for clothes. The heat is so intense that a thin cotton garment becomes a burden hardly to be borne ; and even thus clad the coolies are in a perpetual state of perspiration, which oozes from every pore of their bodies.

The natives are low of stature, dark-skinned, with short, black hair, worn in the same fashion by men and women alike, brushed straight from their foreheads. They have large, bright eyes that might in anger emit sparks, and sometimes flash to no good purpose. These people would be called fairly good-looking but for their filthy habit of chewing betel. I know of no natives in the world who have not formed some unnatural habit, either of chewing or taking stimulants. Tobacco, opium, betelnut, strong drink, or some equivalent, are used by all conditions of humanity, each bringing physical weakness and moral degradation. The Siamese is a slave to the betelnut, which grows on a tall tree very much like the cocoanut palm in appearance, though in girth much less. There is the same clustering of leaves at the top, among which the nuts grow in a large bunch like bananas. They are about the size of an English walnut, and are gathered while still immature.

When mixed with other ingredients and spread on a green leaf they are taken to the market-place for sale. It is safe to say everybody, from the king down, chews the betelnut. It is impossible to disguise the fact, for by its use the lips and teeth become so discolored that these otherwise passably good-looking people are rendered disgusting in appearance. The lips become brown and swollen, and the teeth per· fectly black and covered with a thick coating.

The men and women dress much alike, and two garments are the extent of their limited wardrobe ; for the common people possess no more than the clothes they have on. These garments are simply two straight pieces of cloth woven in the dimensions in which they are worn. The first is about a yard and a quarter wide and three yards long. This is wound about the body and brought up between the thighs, and forms a substitute for trousers. It is adjusted without either hooks, buttons, pins, or fastenings of any kind ; a peculiar twist, that no one seems able to imitate, prevents it from falling off. This "garment" is worn day and night. Another strip forms the cover for the upper part of the body. It is brought across the back under the arms to the front, and there tied or twisted. This leaves the arms and shoulders entirely exposed. When the heat of the country is taken into consideration, this simplicity of dress is to be envied. I groaned beneath a burden of clothes known only in civilized lands, and found life and clothes alike a torment. But these simple children of nature were so clad that they experienced no discomfort even in the hottest sun.

The women are in the most enslaved condition of any women in the world. They have neither legal nor social status, and not one of them could own a paper of pins in her own right. Every woman is branded on the wrist to show to which branch of the imperial family she belongs; and if a man becomes involved in debt, he pawns his wife to pay the bill. She enters service and works until the amount is paid, then goes home to him again.

CHAPTER III.

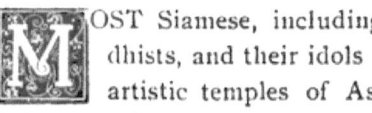OST Siamese, including the king, are Buddhists, and their idols are set up in the most artistic temples of Asia. The architecture belongs entirely to this country. The buildings are high, with arched and curved roofs of fantastic design. The roof is formed of three rows of eaves, extending one below the other. These are finished with highly colored porcelain, cut in various shapes, and at the edge rows of small bells, said to be of gold, are placed a few feet apart. These are so light that the wind sets them tinkling, and a sweet ripple of music is borne out on the breeze that can be heard for some distance.

In one of these buildings sleeps in endless repose the great Buddha, the largest idol in the world. The temple itself is a splendid structure, the most beautiful of all the two hundred in Bangkok. The high tiled roof comes to an abrupt point, and from each side extends the square finishings. The sides are gilded and inlaid with cut glass of various colors, in the shape of diamonds, presenting a gorgeous appearance where the roof peeps out from among the feathery foliage. In different parts of the interior stand life-sized images with one hand placed over the

The Sleeping Buddha, Siam.

'र

breast and the other raised, as if in solemn warning
to the passer-by. The central figure in the temple
is the great sleeping idol. Its position is recumbent,
the head resting upon one hand. The idol extends
almost the whole length of the temple. It is built
of masonry, covered with gold leaf, and is one hundred and forty feet long, and forty feet through the
thickest part of the body. Its feet are five yards
long, and its toes one yard. On its toe-nails are
inscribed the virtues of Buddha, ten in number. The
soles are inlaid with designs in mother-of-pearl,
beaten bronze and chased gold, which represent
the various transmigrations of Buddha.

At the time of my visit the place presented a somewhat weird scene. The temple is closed at night by
great wooden shutters put up at the long windows.
Toward evening, just as the last rays of the setting
sun lingered on the roof-spires and hilltops, I entered
the temple, which was somewhat darkened by the
partly closed shutters. Going around to the front of
the idol, I saw a woman and child burning a small
taper before this huge image. It was indeed a
strange scene : the great idol lying in endless rest ;
the dimly burning taper ; the day, slowly dying from
the heavens, casting its last fading light on this hideous monster, and touching it with a softness that
would feign have warmed it into something better.

My guide, standing near one of the great pillars,
knocked softly upon it with his cane, and from the
dome flew hundreds of bats that had sought shelter
in the darkness. What a picture ! The bats, with

rustling wings, making the unearthly sound that
nothing but these creatures know how to make ; the
faint light of the incense ; and the glow of the sink
ing sun falling upon the kneeling mother and child,
and casting their shadows upon the painted idol – a
scene most pathetic.   The mother took the small
hands of the child — a sweet-looking, innocent little
creature — placed their palms together, and brought
them to the floor ; then for a moment rested the
child's head upon them, teaching it a prayer to the
idol.

The Siamese seem to be a very intelligent people,
but their form of worship is anything but in keeping
with even an ordinary degree of intellect.   One can
easily understand how minds, darkened by superstition, can "imagine vain things" and worship spirits,
or how the splendor and majesty of the rising and
setting sun can attract devotion ; but to see rational
beings prostrate themselves before piles of wood or
stone, no matter how thickly gilded or richly attired,
expecting by heart-cries and protests to be delivered
from disaster, passes all comprehension.   These people believe in the transmigration of the soul ; having
lived once on earth, they expect to live again as a
chicken, cow, bird or insect, in a higher or lower
state of being, according to the merit they have made
during their life.   Their whole religion is a system of
merit-making.   The distress of an animal moves
them to hasty action for its relief; not that they are
touched by its suffering, but because the opportunity
is presented for making merit.

I was once crossing the river in a small boat in which some chickens were being taken over. The heat was great, and beat down upon the poor things until they began to pant. The boatman could not leave his oars, but he said to a companion, "Give the chickens some water and make some merit for me." No pity for the poor, thirsty fowl—only anxiety to benefit himself. It is because of their belief in transmigration that these people refrain from eating flesh in any form. In taking the life of a chicken or other animal they would stand in fear of having killed their grandmother or some other worthy ancestor.

CHAPTER IV.

HE ruler of Siam, Prow Chula Chum Clow by name, is a most intelligent man who speaks three different languages and has quite a knowledge of the outside world. The present king is the first ruler who ever left his domain. Some time ago he paid a visit to Singapore, and the citizens of that town erected a statue of an elephant in the public square in commemoration of his visit. The king is more progressive than the previous rulers, but he is slow to bring changes to his people or adopt new methods. With few exceptions the same usages prevail that have been handed down through the centuries. Some small changes have been made, but nothing that indicates a spirit of real progress. It has ever been an unwritten law that the royal family must marry royalty. As they have been largely shut up to themselves, and have had, practically, no dealings with the outside world, the lack of opportunity has prevented them from intermarrying in the royalty of surrounding countries, after the European fashion. Because of this the king's choice in marriage is limited to a selection from his own family. The late king, like the present one, had many wives and children; from the children of his father the present king

chose his wife. They are half brother and sister, both
children of the late ruler by different wives. The
recognized royal children are those of the queen only,
who occupies the palace with the king. These children are five in number, and the oldest has been proclaimed heir-apparent. Besides these the king is the
happy father of forty other children. In his harem it
is said there are fifteen hundred women who are all
of more or less noble birth, for only the noble may
venture to send their daughters to the king. The
highest possible honor that can be bestowed upon a
man is the addition of his sweet young daughter to
the hundreds of women who live within the palace
grounds.

The king lives in great state in a very large palace.
The building is of white stone, two or three stories
high, and of modern architecture. The great steps
are guarded by two immense elephants, built of brick
and mortar and covered with gold leaf. When the
king leaves the palace he is accompanied by all the
pomp usual among more enlightened rulers. His
stables are the finest in Asia. He scorns the little
Indian pony, and his horses are brought from the
country that produces the king of horse-flesh—Australia. His charger is black as coal, with fiery eyes,
and is an "up-to-date" high-stepper. Besides this
fine array of some hundreds of thoroughbred horses,
the king dotes on his three white elephants. These
are seldom used; they are regarded as sacred. The
elephants are carefully cared for by attendants, and
quarters have been built for their special comfort, each

having a large, airy room. In the center of the room
a heavy pillar is decorated with a canopy of showy
drapery, under which the vicious creature paws, aims
ineffective blows at his innocent keeper, and otherwise displays to the looker-on his appreciation of the
care bestowed upon him.

The day was appointed on which I was to feast my
eyes upon the visage of a real live king. I had little
fear, for I had passed through a similar experience, and
had come off with my life. It is the custom to appear
before his majesty in full dress ; that is, in some kind
of light dress, with gloves, etc. I was traveling at
the time with no other baggage than a valise, in
which limited space I could not stow away a whole
dry-goods store ; so in matters of dress I had really
small choice. The garment settled upon was dragged
forth into the sunlight for an airing, and next day I
was on my way to the palace. A long row in a small
boat on a sweltering day, with my clothes clinging
closer than glue, and my front hair drooping—in
fact, almost dripping—were the penalties of going to
see the king.

I reached the outer walls of the grounds, where
two noblemen met me and escorted me to the corridor
of the palace. There I met the high and mighty of
the land, waiting to perform the arduous task of presenting me to the king. A number of foreign representatives were expecting to be received, and these
were also present in the elegant corridor, where we
were served with refreshments while waiting. Presently a message came from the king, through the

prince, his eldest brother, that his majesty was prepared to receive me. The prince was to escort me to
the audience-room and present me. He offered his
arm and conducted me to a long hall, on each side of
which stood armed soldiers ; this led to the private
audience-room of the king. Great bronzed doors
opened as we approached, and when I entered the
king walked half way across the room to greet me,
which was really done in a most democratic way ; he
then motioned me to a seat near by.

The king speaks English, but never to a foreigner
in the palace. I, of course, spoke my own language,
which he understood perfectly, though he carried his
part of the conversation in Siamese, and his older
brother interpreted. He was thoroughly informed on
the latest phases of the woman question, and seemed
to know of all the efforts that were being put forth by
them for their own elevation and the betterment of the
world. When I spoke to him of the education of his
own women, many of whom had never attended
school, he was of the opinion that the time had not
yet come for general education among the Siamese.
His argument was clever, considered *ex parte*. He
first touched upon a thought that has awakened
wide-spread interest in connection with the higher
education of women ; namely, will it unfit them for
the peculiar conditions that surround them ? In
speaking of this the king said : " With education
there always comes culture and refinement. The
people of this country are very poor. If they become
cultured and refined, they will naturally want things

about them more beautiful than those they have been accustomed to, and this education will bring with it a spirit of discontent."

There may be something in the king's argument, but I am of the opinion that he is fully aware of one fact : If the women of Siam ever become educated he can never build walls high enough to keep fifteen hundred women in his harem.

After an hour of pleasant conversation, during which I gathered his majesty's ideas on many local and foreign subjects, I left the palace with a guide who was under instructions to show me around the building and grounds.

JAVA AND BURMAH.

CHAPTER I.

THE GRAND TEMPLE OF JAVA.

AT THE present rate of "globe trotting" the press of time is so great that very few find leisure to depart from the beaten paths of travel, and consequently some of the places of greatest interest are missed; but when one starts with six, seven or more years before him, many byways and side-tracks lead the pilgrim to spots almost unknown. Among these, is the island of Java, and it is well worth the traveler's while to spend an extra month, if need be, to reach the center of that country and see what should be classed among the wonders of the world.

Were Java under the rule of any but the sleepy Hollanders—who are still more sleepy for their sojourn there—the center of the island would long ago have been made more accessible, and the people brought in closer contact with the outside world. But when Holland, after the manner of other countries, took unto herself this land, pensioned the rulers, set aside all native rights, and appropriated the labor of the natives to cultivate and make rich the soil, she lost sight of all things save the enrichment of her treasury, and the bestowal of "fat offices" upon a few favored individuals.

In the way of vegetation Java contains all that we imagine as belonging to Eden—palms of all kinds, breadfruit, cocoanut, and scores of other tropical trees, as well as spice-plants and fruits, and a general growth more luxuriant of foliage and graceful of form than that found anywhere in the western world. These trees form the home of birds of gorgeous plumage, and fireflies and insects that look like flying gems as they move about in their glory of color. I saw there more than the poet has dreamed of, or painter ever depicted, for nature far outrivals the skill of man. On one side I caught glimpses of pretty little valleys clothed in eternal summer; on the other, lofty mountain peaks crowned with fleecy clouds.

At the Batavia postoffice I read in English, "The grand temple in the interior of Java, that for architectural design, decorations, carvings and finish is worthy of Greece itself, testifies to a cultivation of the natives that has long since died out." It did not take me long to make up my mind to make the trip to the interior, not only that I might gaze upon this triumph of architectural skill, but that I might also see the ruins to be passed on the way.

In looking upon the ruins time has wrought, it seems wonderful how nature reclaims and draws again within the earth all that has been taken out

A Javanese Home.

of it. Seeds are dropped by birds, or blown by the wind between the joints of stone ; moistened by the rains and fed by the dust, they germinate, spread their roots, force even the mighty stones asunder and throw them to the ground whence they were dug. Everywhere in Java the destroying vegetation is throwing down, feeding upon and covering up ruins that, for want of a little care, will soon be lost to sight.

The journey to the temple is two hundred miles by slow rail, with all the annoyances experienced in that hot clime,—dust flying, perspiration oozing from every pore in the body, and clothes a burden almost unendurable. The two hundred miles covered, the really difficult part of the journey began by stage. The six little horses were changed every few miles, and even then I felt that a humane society should have had charge of the whole party ; but we rode, struggled and walked until we reached our journey's end, where I sat down to refresh myself on the cocoa-nuts brought by one of the coolies. If the distance had been twice as long, and the difficulties even more numerous, I would have felt that the stupendous sight before me was sufficient requital for all the discomfort. The legend given by the natives describes the temple and its construction better than I could bring it before the reader.

Two thousand years ago, the natives decided to erect a great temple worthy of their country and religion. A site was first selected in the interior of the island, on a gently sloping hill, where a structure that would abide all time should stand. A plan was then called for, and the scores submitted must have outnumbered the glory-seeking aspirants to honor who would have figured in architectural fame at the World's Fair. In that country where the common people have no political rights, but where the high places are held by right of birth, it is a strange thing that the plan of this temple should have been submitted to a popular vote, and thus decided. The sound of chisel or hammer was not to be heard on the temple. Every stone was finished at the quarry, and the whole was to be placed without mortar or cement. Masons, builders, sculptors, and workmen of all kinds engaged in the great work, and for many years thousands labored from sunrise until sunset. One massive stone after another was dug from the quarry, and under the skillful hand of the sculptor was converted into a thing of beauty, and sent to fill its place in the pile that was to form the temple. The time came when the last figure stood out in all its beauty upon the last block ; the cap-stone had been polished with care, and all was in readiness to pile the stones one upon another, a task which was to be completed in three days. One hundred thousand workmen came from all parts of the island, ready to complete the work ; a national holiday was proclaimed, and two million pilgrims came to see the structure reared.

I stood on a great knoll, and as I viewed the landscape on all sides, the scenes of that distant time came clearly before me. For three days rose this temple of Boer Buddha, without the sound of ham-

Javanese Child.   Javanese Fruit Woman.

mer—as mute as are the workings of nature. The majestic pile rose in all its perfection of form. The temple was built in terraces five feet high and four feet in width, until it rose to the height of three hundred feet. Illuminated by the last rays of a gorgeous eastern sunset, the cap-stone was placed. A signal was given, and the vast multitude bowed in silent adoration.

The temple stands to-day almost as complete as when left by the workmen, and will probably remain only to crumble when time itself shall fade.

CHAPTER II.

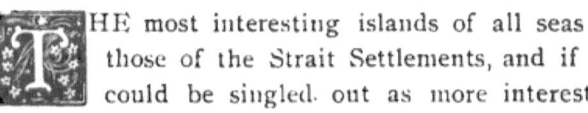

THE most interesting islands of all seas are those of the Strait Settlements, and if one could be singled out as more interesting than another, because of its people, I should name the small island of Singapore. It is only fourteen miles across, and sixty miles long ; yet in the streets of Singapore thirty different languages are spoken. In the beautiful harbor float the flags of all nations, and it would be difficult to point out a place that forms a more impressive scene than that witnessed from the bay.

The European population consists chiefly of merchants, government officials, military men and a few missionaries. The island is almost on the equator, and because of its situation the climate is very trying. A garment the weight of a mosquito-net becomes a burden, and the effort in using a fan produces the greatest discomfort. Servants are numerous in each household, and the white people do little beyond "breathing the breath of life " ; this I am sure they would not do if they could hire a servant to do it for them. If one wants to grow lazy gracefully, Singapore is the place to go. The natives are the laziest people in the world. The Indian bullocks, used as

beasts of burden, have a dreamy, far-away look in
their eyes, and step with lazy tread. The native, too
lazy to get up into the cart, sits on the pole between
the animals, his long, thin, black legs dangling in a
most lazy manner. Instead of wasting strength in
urging his lazy beast with a whip, he twists his tail
to remind him that he must move on. The very
breeze fans your cheek with a lazy breath, and you
settle down, glad to do nothing—in short, to be lazy.

Standing one morning on the steps of the postoffice
I spent an hour in watching the passing multitude.
They came trooping by, of every shade of skin, speaking many strange tongues, and dressed in every color
and variety of costume. The ever-present John Chinaman, from the mandarin of great wealth, with his
fine horses, magnificent modern home and costly apparel, to the poor, miserable coolie who gains a few
pennies a day by making himself a beast of burden,
racing through heat of noonday sun, urged on by
some heartless driver— both classes of the Celestial
Empire form a large portion of the population of the
city. Japan, Siam, Burmah, India, and, in fact, most
of the countries of vast Asia are represented here in
this cosmopolitan corner of the earth.

An individual standing near me attracted my special attention. His make-up and personality were
very striking. He was tall, fully six feet, and thin—
well, it seemed to me that he would need to stand
twice in the sunlight to cast a shadow! His eyes
were sunken ; his nose had a decided crook. On his
head was a wool cap, though the thermometer stood

one hundred and fifteen in the shade. His feet were pushed into a pair of shoes, the toes of which turned over toward the instep and ended in a sharp point. To his ankles fell a loose white garment, over which he wore a green silk robe. His strange looks led me to inquire from what part of the earth he had *escaped.* No one seemed to know.

While in Singapore, an invitation came to visit Jahore, a southern extremity of Hindustan, separated from Singapore only by a narrow passage of water. The road which led to the water's edge was perfect. It was cut through a dense jungle, and tracts on each side had been cleared and planted with coffee and cocoanut groves; but much still remained a wild growth, where vines and runners had overgrown the trees and become tangled in endless confusion, presenting a scene of wondrous beauty. Three hours ride over this road brought us to a small boat in waiting, and a few moments later I was in the sultan's carriage, on my way to see something of royalty in the far East.

The sultan's domain is small, and the population mixed—a few whites, some Chinese, and a few thousand Malays. The sultan lives in great state, and is very much given to display. He is low of stature, heavy-set, with dark eyes, and a great growth of white hair. Being a Mohammedan, he never removes his hat, which, when I saw him, was of foreign make.

One of the most interesting things concerning royal personages is that after all they are just like other people—with the same emotions and sentiments, and given to romance in common with the rest of the human family. On the occasion of the sultan's last visit to England he traveled as a private person, under the name of Albert Barker. He met a young lady while abroad, for whom he formed a strong attachment, or at least he thought he did. He proposed that she return with him, and become the fair sultana of his realm. She favored the idea, and exercised a woman's privilege by saying " Yes." Time wore on, and the sultan exercised a man's privilege by changing his mind, and left the fair maiden with more damaged affections than she could manage : whereupon she sued His Serene Highness for fifty thousand dollars. The case was tried in the English courts, and it was decided that as the sultan was a reigning monarch he was beyond jurisdiction. There are many advantages in being a "reigning monarch."

The palace in which the sultan entertains his foreign guests is furnished in European style, with modern accessories. The dining-room is especially well arranged, and most gorgeous in furnishings. The walls are finished in panels, the alternate ones of looking-glass. The floor is of pure white marble, mosaiced in richly colored stones, and here and there Turkish rugs give a showy oriental touch to the room. But the most lavish display is to be seen at the table. While in England the sultan bought a dinner service of solid gold, and his foreign guests look upon something rarely seen either in the eastern or western world.

Through some mistake respecting the hour of return, the carriage failed to meet me, and my only means of reaching Singapore was by jinrickisha, drawn by Chinese coolies. Seated in this miniature carriage, a coolie jumped between the shafts and started down the road with alarming speed. The sun was on the decline, the heavy shadows fell across the road, affording cooling shade, and the coolies trotted steadily on, bringing us to our destination in less time than that consumed in the morning's drive.

CHAPTER III.

T WOULD be supposed that any sort of accommodation could be secured from Singapore, where can be seen almost every kind of craft that is propelled by steam, sailed by canvas, or sent gliding down the bay by the strong hand of the native; but in traveling along all the eastern coasts it is almost impossible to find comfortable quarters on the steamers. It was my unhappy fate to take passage on a Dutch steamer. As usual the discomfort of seasickness was upon me, and I was unable to go on deck for a few days. When I encountered the captain he informed me that the ship had been ordered to Sumatra to convey the fever-stricken troops to the mainland. For many years the Dutch and the people of one end of this island have been at war over a small strip of land. I suppose thousands of Holland's sons have died of fever, or perished in arms, during the time since the first war, to say nothing of the natives whose lives have been sacrificed in defense of their country. The prospect of sailing for a few days with a fever-stricken crew was anything but pleasant, but as the open sea afforded no desirable means of escape I settled down and decided, as one must so often do in tramping the earth, to make the best of it.

The Sumatran port was reached about midnight, and the ship dropped anchor only long enough to take on the troops. No one was allowed to go ashore. As we anchored no sight or sound of troops was seen or heard ; but presently, borne on the wings of the breeze, came notes of martial music. As it approached nearer and nearer, we heard the steady tramp of feet, and in a short time the soldiers were all aboard. Those who were able to walk, marched on board ; others, in the more advanced stages of the disease, were carried ; and the steamer put to sea again, all drawing a breath of relief and none fearing the fever, which was not contagious.

We sailed next day over smooth waters, amid spice islands, the air heavy with pungent odors and the perfume of flowers, until the sun of that day faded behind the beauty of an island, and evening was upon us. The soft twilight shades soon lengthened into darkness ; then the pale moon rose and threw a weird light over the scene ; one great star after another spangled the heavens, and night swept on. The steamer's lights were turned low, and " tired nature's sweet restorer " had come to some on board. But on the lower deck weary eyes refused to close, and were filled with tears of sorrow ; men moved about with noiseless tread and almost hushed breath, giving orders in an undertone. An officer came to where I was seated on the deck—the heat of the cabin had become unendurable—and said, " Some of the sol-

Sumatra Woman.

diers have died, and must be buried at sea. We shall slack up at midnight and put them overboard ; don't be disturbed.''

What a night that was ! one never to be forgotten. I sat alone, dreading the midnight hour. Soon the steamer moved slower and slower. I put my hands to my ears and closed my eyes, thinking to shut out every sight and sound ; but soon I heard a great splash, then another and another, until almost a score had been consigned to a watery grave. The last brave soldier who died had asked that the flag of his country might form his winding-sheet. His comrades, many of whom had fought and suffered with him, carried out his dying request. The flag of Holland was wound about him, and tenderly they lifted him to the plank ; I heard another splash and the steamer moved on. There can be nothing more distressing than a burial at sea. On the Dutch ship no service was read or prayer offered ; it was simply a matter of casting overboard.

The next morning we gathered at the table, but no word of the sad scene was spoken. It was a thing of the past, and the pressing duties of the hour had driven it out of our thoughts. In this changeful world of ours, joy and sorrow are ever crowding upon each other; the tear is soon dried and gives way to a smile, or a smile quickly passes to give place to a tear—and the old world rolls on just the same.

I became engaged in conversation with the captain, who was a true son of Holland, but spoke English well. He at once took me for one who had wandered

from the land of the stars and stripes. Just how he
was able to locate me I am unable to say—probably
by my good looks! I found him the most profane
man I had ever met in my life ; in fact, he seemed to
have determined to punctuate every sentence he uttered with profanity. I was the only lady passenger,
but he swore in conversing with me just as he did in
talking to the men. Finally I said, " Captain, why
do you swear so ? " The man opened his eyes in
utter astonishment, and said, " Why, did I swear?
If I did, I assure you I did not know it." He was
most profuse in his apologies, and begged I would
not consider it a lack of respect for a lady.

With the echo of oaths reaching my ears from time
to time, we sailed on until we reached the shores of
Burmah, that country whose native government was
recently overthrown by force of arms, and which thus
became part of the vast posessions of British India.

The Burmese government was purely despotic—the
king sentenced to imprisonment, torture or death,
according to his pleasure, without trial, or the least
pretence to justice. Everything connected with the
king was said to be " golden." When he went into
the streets a fence six feet high was erected on each
side, that none of the common people might look
upon his " golden presence." King Thebaw's grandfather had a spear which he often threw at those who
offended him, but his son is said never to have killed
anyone, though he has thrown the spear several
times. Under the Burmese government there were
the most minute regulations concerning the construc-

A Burmese Girl.

tion of houses, wearing of ornaments, and manner of dress. For a violation of these customs severe punishment was meted out to the offender. There were also special regulations concerning the manufacture of umbrellas ; they must be of a certain size, color and texture. The king used white ; other dignitaries carried umbrellas of different colors, according to the order of the king.

Mandalay, the capital, is situated in upper Burmah, and is reached from Rangoon by rail. This old historic town has often been the theater of scenes that have greatly affected the nation, both for good and evil. Here the British made their way to the palace, and, after having dethroned the king, proclaimed Burmah a British possession. But perhaps the scenes witnessed here, that have left the deepest impress upon the people, were those in the days when the brave Judson made his way to the king and received permission to preach the gospel in the land.

CHAPTER IV.

ANDALAY is a city of great beauty, and contains a palace the like of which has never been erected in any other part of the world. This structure occupies a place in the center of the city. The outermost inclosure consists of a stockade of teakwood posts twenty feet high. Within are three successive inclosures of brick walls, beyond which stands the palace, made of carved teakwood. This wood is most remarkable; it is said to almost rival stone in withstanding the test of time. As the Burmese excel in carving, the beauty of the palace is beyond description. Since the British have taken possession a part of the palace has been converted into offices, other parts into a church, and the chief portion has been reserved as the governor's residence.

The city is reached both by rail and water, so I decided to return by water. The sun was intense, and the reflected heat from the water much greater than the heat on land ; but the beauty of the landscape repaid us for the endurance of the tropical sun. On each side, the same foliage that marks the tropics the world over lent its charm to the scene. Between the long, swaying branches of the cocoanut or palm I caught glimpses of the huts of the natives and their

places of worship ; for go where you will in Asia the
ever-present temple, in all its varied forms, stands
out as the feature of the landscape. This is also true
of Burmah, especially as one nears Rangoon and sees
the " Great Pagoda of Burmah " lift its head some
three hundred feet above its surroundings.

It would be difficult indeed to describe this wonder,
which has been standing for more than two thousand
years. The pagoda is built on a rise of land covering some acres ; it is solid, cone-shaped—diminishing
in rounded outlines—and surmounted by an umbrella
spire, covered with gold leaf to the very point.
Flight after flight of stairs lead to the elevation
where the place of worship is built. All about the
grounds are small archways, temples, and all manner
of fantastic-shaped shelters for the hundreds of idols
set up around the pagoda. These are of alabaster,
wood and brass, and have been set up by devout
worshipers as works of merit. They are in every
possible attitude—reclining, sitting cross-legged and
standing—all representing the founder of their faith,
Gautama, commonly called Buddha. The fingers
and toes are all the same length—a special mark of
beauty. The lobe of the ear extends until it reaches
the shoulders, and the face is gross in the extreme.

A remarkable feature of eastern life is seen in every
city and hamlet throughout the many countries that
go to make up the vast continent of Asia. The rich
of these lands spend great sums of money erecting
places of shelter for their ugly gods, and leave their
own fellow-creatures to the most abject poverty, a

prey to the greatest hardships and suffering. This
was most noticeable in visiting the pagoda. At
the foot of the steps, and along the sides up to the
landing sat scores of those unfortunate creatures so
numerous in the East—lepers. There they were, old
and young, disfigured and defaced, bearing marks of
the awful disease in all parts of their bodies. As
the richly dressed worshiper lifted his silken robes to
prevent contact with the stone steps, he paid no attention to the misery of the beggars, but as their cries of,
"Oh, rich man, give us rice for to-day?" rose higher
and higher, the "rich man" only hastened on to
satisfy his conscience by sacrificing flowers or burning
incense before his favorite god, when the money thus
spent would have provided for one sufferer for a
day, perhaps for several days.

I turned from this scene of suffering to hasten to
the wharf where the outgoing steamer on which I was
to be a passenger was anchored. My destination wa :
Maulmem, a seaport city only a few hours ride from
Rangoon. This is an old, historical city, full of interest. But as the Irishman said of Naples, "The
greatest wonders of Naples are outside of it," so the
most interesting features of this place are outside of
it." Toward the objects of interest we turned our
faces one day, and truly went up through "trials and
tribulations." In traveling in these countries the
great discomfort is the necessity of taking provisions,
servants, carriages, boats, and no end of "extras"
that must make up part of the luggage. All these
difficulties were finally overcome, and we took an

early start and drove down to the water's edge, where
we had to be ferried across in a native canoe. This
was not a matter of simply stepping from the carriage
to the boat ; someone had to manage the taking over
of the provisions ; but after many soul-harrowing ex·
periences we finally reached the other side, where a
two-wheeled cart, drawn by Indian bullocks, was in
waiting to convey us to our journey's end. Six of us
got up into the cart, sat tailor-fashion on the straw in
the bottom, and off we started. We had scarcely
reached the edge of the village before we found that
the pitiless tropical sun was no respecter of persons,
but beat down on us in dreadful fury. We decided
to make an awning of the linen laprobe, so a halt was
called, and branches of distant trees were brought
over and made into poles to uphold the " awning "
at the four corners of the cart. This served every
purpose, and we were protected from the heat of the
sun, which had now become dangerous.

Driving over the plains of India in a two-wheeled
bullock-cart is anything but pleasant ; but as "everything comes to an end," so did our journey, and we
camped on the shady side of a great lone mountain in
the center of a wide plain. On this mountain were
the famous caves we intended to visit. They were
discovered some centuries ago, and a pious-minded
Burmese conceived the idea of laying up an unusual
amount of " merit " by turning the caves into a great
temple. The dome was a natural one, but workmen
were sent for and directed to " improve " the beauty
of nature by carving in the solid rock hundreds of

small images of Buddha. This done, other idols were built. We saw one great one stretched full length, lying on its back. It was built of bricks covered with mortar and finished with gold leaf, and it was minus an arm and a foot: In other chambers were larger and smaller idols, some of metals, others of wood.

We had brought with us torches of white and blue lights to aid in our inspection of the caves. These ignited we started on a tour of investigation, the party dividing as inclination led. Going into one chamber I was amazed to find one of our company with her dust-robe on the ground, looking around for a god that pleased her most. Soon one of the drivers emerged from the darkest corner loaded with a great mass of stone supposed to represent the physical beauty of the founder of his faith. This was carefully rolled up in the dust-robe and sent to the cart as a souvenir of the trip. Similar scenes confronted us as we went from room to room, and when we prepared for the return trip it was a serious question of who should go in the carts, the gods or the party. Finally, it was decided that everyone who had taken an idol must sit on it, and thus economize space. Be it forever recorded that I did not ride home *sitting on a god.*

INDIA.

CHAPTER I.

TO THE BOTTOM OF THE SEA.

 HUNDRED and fifty thousand miles of travel by land and sea affords great scope for a diversity of experiences. If one were to ask me where I had had the greater variety—on land or sea—I would be unable to say, for both have brought such varied experiences that at times the tears would unbidden start, and again I would be almost convulsed with laughter. Occasionally, terror, also, has had almost complete possession of me.

I believe the most remarkable experience in all my journeys occurred at sea. I had been traveling through the Australasian colonies, and was on my way to India. There is little traffic up that coast, and the steamers are anything but first-class—simply cargo-boats, with passenger cabins. We started from Freemantle, on the west coast. The passengers were few in number; six traveling men, one minister, a French catholic priest and myself made up the list. The whole coast is a wilderness of sand-hills. As far as the eye can reach no sign of vegetation is to be

seen save a growth of wild flowers ; these belong to
the everlasting family, are of every hue and shade,
and, strangely enough, take root in the burning sand,
among the rocks, and on the barren hillsides. At
this time not a drop of rain had fallen in two years.
The sheep and cattle lay dead on the plains by thousands, and the few remaining inhabitants were sick
at heart and discouraged.

On this coast are some of the greatest pearl fish-
eries in the world. Just out at sea, anchored in the
shallow waters, was a fleet of about one hundred and
fifty small boats, manned by twelve or fifteen hundred
men of many nationalities; some were from the Strait
Settlements, and others from Japan and the North.
Our steamer remained here for two days. It is the
custom when a steamer calls at this port for the officers of the pearling fleet to come on board and dine
with the captain. I chanced to sit near one of the
officers. He described the manner of going down to
the bottom of the sea, and concluded by asking,
"Why don't you go down?" He uttered this in a
tone that indicated a challenge, and at the same time
seemed to say, "You dare not go."

When I remembered how tall I was, the thought
came to me, "Surely, they will never have clothes
large enough for me ; " so I replied, "Yes, I will go,
if you have a suit that will fit me." The captain
became so excited that he at once left the dinner-
table, took a skiff, rode over to a pearling-boat, and
in a few moments returned to say that everything was
in readiness. To retreat would be unworthy of my

country, so with trembling limbs and almost bated breath, I started, in company with the stewardess and captain, for the pearling-boat. Here the stewardess helped me prepare for the dive. Two suits of heavy knit wear were soon donned ; then came the outside garment that covered the whole body, all but the hands and head ; a metal hoop was placed around my neck ; on this were a number of screws over which the neck of the dress was pulled ; then came a man with a wrench and made fast each screw. The shoes were next brought out; they weighed thirty-two pounds. When they told me that, I knew I would not stretch them out of shape. Next came the arrangement for the head. This was a sort of helmet, in which were three glass globes, one in front and one on each side, so that the wearer could view his surroundings in all directions. It was adjusted as a cone is screwed on a lamp, and produced a most disagreeable sensation. To the helmet was attached one end of a rubber hose, the other end leading to the air-pump, and arrangements were completed when I put on the weights (forty pounds of lead) about my neck and shoulders.

Thus attired, it was impossible to move, but a number of gentlemen from our steamer, with the gallantry that characterizes their sex throughout the world, offered to put me overboard. It took about ten men to carry me to the side of the ship, and I was thrown overboard—yes, thrown overboard ! I landed on my back, and in a few moments, through the glass of the helmet, I saw those ponderous shoes begin to come up, and I knew I was going down head first. I pulled the signal, and was soon taken on deck, where the surplus air was let out. I was then lowered to the bed of the ocean.

The sensation is very much the same as that experienced in the descent in an elevator. It was just after a wild storm, and the disturbed condition of the water made the occasion not very favorable for sight-seeing. I found the bottom hard and sandy. The water being so much heavier than the suit, I was able to walk about with ease. I did not venture beyond the ends of the boat, though I could see some distance farther. All around me were shells of many colors, seaweed and sponge. The seaweed was filled with pretty red seeds. After a few moments below I pulled the signal-rope and was taken up to the deck of the steamer, none the worse for my trip to the bottom of the sea.

In a few days we reached Singapore, and after a short delay boarded the steamer bound for India. A flood of thought came upon me as I turned my face towards this wonderful land. All the ideas of my childhood concerning it were brought to mind; I recalled pictures I had seen of cruel mothers throwing their children to the crocodiles, and poor, helpless widows cast upon the funeral pile to be burned alive. I wondered if I should see such awful things, but when I reached there, I soon learned that all the horrors ever conceived by human mind were as nothing compared with what I really witnessed.

CHAPTER II.

OUR point of landing was Calcutta, anything but a native city. The whites are found here in such numbers that the whole city has a western appearance. It is full of interest, however. I visited Thackeray's birthplace; the room where Macaulay wrote his wonderful essays; the church where Carey first preached, and the baptistery where Judson was baptized. I then went out to see the native town.

It was at a very good time to visit the outlying city, for the "holy fathers" were just making a pilgrimage to the Hoogly, one of the sacred rivers of India. These men belong to the Brahmin faith, and are supposed to be absolutely holy; their whole time is given up to religious rites—reading holy books and saying long prayers hour after hour. We walked some distance out from the city to their camp, where about twenty were engaged in devotions. They wore only an apology for clothes; they were supposed to be attired in sackcloth and ashes—chiefly ashes. Their hair, which had turned a yellowish color from long contact with ashes, either hung down their backs in uncombed strings, or was twisted around their heads, Chinese style.

In another camp we saw a large company who had come miles, crawling snake fashion; they had trav-

eled over rocks, stumps and stones till their flesh was
bleeding and torn, and the dust had settled in their
hair and eyes till they bore little resemblance to
human beings.

As I went through the city I saw, here and there,
some who were enjoying their "merit-making" to
themselves. One was dragging after him three hundred pounds of chains fastened to his wrists and
ankles. The weight had worn the flesh away and
the bare bones were exposed. Another was lying on
planks driven full of spikes. This had been his resting-place till his whole body was bruised and bleeding. But I think the worst thing I saw was a man
with his hand over his head; he had held it so long
in that position that it was impossible to move it. I
could hardly believe this, but my interpreter, who
was a prince, said, "I have told him you wish to take
hold of his arm to try to move it." I took hold of
it, and might as well have tried to move the arm of a
marble statue; it had become fixed in its position.
His hand was closed, and where the nail of the first
finger touched the flesh, between the thumb and fore-
finger, it had grown through. The nail of the thumb
was several inches long. For all this torture they
expect to live in a higher life when they go through
the next transmigration.

Leaving Calcutta I journeyed northward as far as
Benares, the chief city of the Brahmins. Of all degrading influences that could be imagined, all superstitions indulged in by rational beings, all darkness
that ever clouded the human mind, the sum total is

Serampore College, Scene of Carey's Labors.

centered in this city. Benares is built on one side of
the sacred Ganges, and extends about three miles
along the bank. Early one morning I took a boat and
sailed up and down the river, to better see the city.
All the houses on the banks have steps leading down
into the water, and at this early hour hundreds were
making their way to the sacred stream to bathe, and
worship by throwing sacred flowers into the water.
Almost every act in a Hindu's life is one of devotion. As he descends the steps and dips himself beneath the water, he is happy in the thought that he
has accomplished a twofold purpose — cleansed his
body and paid homage to the stream.

While this was going on at the water's edge, just
above, on the bank, I witnessed scenes never to be
forgotten. The highest hope of the Hindu is to die
in sight of the sacred stream. In one place could
be seen hundreds of men and women afflicted with
every disease that could be named, and in every stage
of death. One old man, in a dying condition, was
being borne to the brink by his friends. They reached
there just as he was about breathing his last, and that
he might know the blessing of a final look at the
river, a young woman rushed to his side, and with
her fingers held his eyelids open until the last spark
of life had fled. This sight of poor, wretched, igno-
rant humanity, as looked upon on that spot, filled
me with a sense of gratitude for the blessing of birth
in a Christian land.

At one edge of the city is a spot set aside for disposing of the dead. It has been the custom of the

Brahmins, so far as we have any record of their methods, to dispose of the dead by burning, and the very primitive way in which this is done makes it seem terrible.

Five or six bodies lay at the river's edge with their feet in the water, while, above, the preparations for disposing of them were in progress. Special men are engaged, who go at their work very much as they would in building a house. Four heavy iron rods are driven in the ground, about six feet apart one way and four the other. Logs of wood are piled up on this space to a height of about four feet, the remains are placed on the pile, and other wood makes the pyre complete. Sitting or standing near are the numerous hired mourners and the relatives. They are dressed in pure white, and wail and howl ; the one who can make the most noise is the best mourner. The nearest relative, who is the chief mourner, touches off the funeral pyre, the wailing is renewed, and, to add to the confusion, boys beat tom-toms (drums) and "play" on all sorts of instruments that produce unearthly sounds. The whole scene is far beyond description. The long flights of stairs leading into the stream, crowded with bathers repeating prayers, the dead and dying, the cry of beggars, the wail of mourners, the awful sound of the music, the cracking of the fire, and the dark clouds of curling smoke, all made a bewildering, confusing scene from which I was glad to turn, only to find things equally shocking.

Mounting the stone steps, I soon reached the streets of the city, and found my way to the leading temples.

The first was the Monkey Temple. Here hundreds
of these creatures are cared for and almost worshiped
by the natives, who regard them as sacred. My next
visit was to the Cow Temple. The cow is also held
a sacred animal by these people, and this temple, set
aside for their special care, is of real oriental splendor
and design, highly ornamented inside and out. The
lower floor is set aside for the cows, and I found it
just like an ordinary stable, only special care is bestowed upon the animals. Hundreds of worshipers
visit the place daily. At one end is a shrine for the
only image the Brahmins have. It represents three
gods in one, and is the most hideous thing that could
possibly be imagined. Worshipers come early in the
morning with young kids to sacrifice to this god.
The poor little creatures are tied up by the hind legs,
hung against the wall, their throats cut, and their
blood thrown before the idol ; then the worshiper
bathes in the Ganges near by. The noise, talk, running and pushing against each other, and the absence
of all influences that lead to a worshipful frame of
mind, are the most noticeable features of the lower
part of the temple. The upper part is set aside for
women who are married to the god, which means that
they are set aside as the special property of the holy
fathers. These women are either widows—the despised of India—or young girls who have been sold
by parents whose love for money is greater than their
love for their children. ·

CHAPTER III.

HEN I reached India I found it a much larger country than I had expected, and I was surprised to learn that I could go from the most southerly city to the northern boundary by rail. The journey is a long and very tiresome one ; it cannot be taken in comfort unless one supplies his own bed. This necessitates a servant, and endless trouble in making your needs known. But finally the great plains were crossed, and I reached Peshawar at the gateway to Afghanistan. This is a very curious city, unlike any other place in India. The old city is surrounded by a high wall with sixteen gates, all of which are closed by nine o'clock, after which no one is admitted without countersigns and passwords.

Within the walls of this city there are only four white people ; these are all young women from England in charge of the Woman's Hospital. Their house is surrounded by walls about forty feet high, and the gateway is guarded by armed sepoys. In leaving the hospital to drive, walk, or visit a patient, the young ladies always go under escort. I went to the top of the house to view the city and surroundings. The houses are peculiar to this place—built of sun-dried bricks and plastered over with mud. Around the top of each house is built lattice-work, through which the women of the family may look

234

Traveling in Bombay.

unseen into the streets below. They bring their
spinning to this place, and in small groups work and
chatter the days away.

Driving through the city I saw a very different race
of people from those in central and southern India.
The city is cosmopolitan, and the frontier people mingle to an extent unknown in any other part of the
country. The natives from Cashmere were especially
interesting, and their dress was peculiar to themselves. The season was winter, and somewhat severe
for that country, so these people were clad in their
warmest garments. The outer were made of goat-
skin, worn fur side in. The long fur coat reached
almost to the ankles, and was belted in at the waist
with a knit scarf. Their boots were of heavy leather,
loose and baggy at the ankles, with upturned toes.
On their heads were cone-shaped skin hats ; these
were also worn hair side in, and the hair hung down
over their foreheads like modern bangs. The whole
make-up gave them a very strange appearance.

The city is chiefly Mohammedan, and early in the
morning, before daylight, can be heard the call to
prayer. A Mohammedan with strong lungs and
heavy voice goes through the city crying, " O sleeper,
arise and pray ; there is but one God and his prophet
is Mohammed ! "

Beyond the city, towards the north, lie the great
plains, shut in by three ranges of mountains—sandy
foot-hills without a shrub or blade of grass, then a
greater elevation, and, finally, the highest range,
covered with a late fall of snow. Through these

ranges of such vast extent, three passes lead to the countries beyond, forming the only means of communication. Of these passes Khyber is most noted. It is the gateway to Afghanistan, that country whose ruler is fearful the whole world will invade his possessions. I determined to at least go through the pass, and the natural perversity of woman's nature filled me with desire to commit the forbidden act— enter his domain.

Arrangements were soon made and I was ready for the journey. The morning was bitterly cold ; white frost had fallen upon everything, and even through my thick robes and wraps I could feel the wintry breeze. A drive of eight miles over a dreary waste such as could never be described, brought us to the fort, which is the end of the Indian possessions. Towering in awful grandeur before us rose the high peaks of the mountain range through which we were to ride thirty miles before the closely guarded territory of the Ameer would be reached. The pass is filled with bandits and outlaws—who live in caverns in the rocks and holes in the earth—making the journey most unsafe. I had applied to the government for troops, and found them in readiness for me at the fort. As they mounted their beautiful horses, most of them white as the snow before us, and rode off, the sight was a pretty one. The natives wore dark blue turbans wound about their heads with the grace known only to these people. Their uniform was of semi-European cut ; dark brown in color, and belted in with dark blue belts. They carried guns, long

Elephant Traveling.

Traveling by Ekka in Cashmere.

swords, and glistening bayonets, and made quite a show. The outriders carried spears.

The pass through which we were to journey was thirty miles long and of perfectly natural formation. Had all the force of dynamite been applied, and years of toil spent in an effort to cut through the range, so perfect a pass could not have been constructed. The road is irregular and winding, and because of the granite walls on each side the highway is somewhat gloomy. On the summits of the lower hills were round houses used as lookout posts, and in these were stationed hundreds of armed sepoys. As soon as a footfall is heard on the road they spring to their posts and in their native tongue cry out, "Traveler, pass on ; you are safe, you are safe."

When half way through we came upon the fort of Ali Masgid. This is situated at an elevation of three thousand feet, and commands a fine view of both entrances to the pass. I made my way to the top to see a caravan coming from Cabool, the capital of Afghanistan. By the aid of the field-glass I could see camels, hundreds strong, little asses weighted down with great burdens, and many Indian cattle. They made their way over the winding road ; now and then a camel would find its way over a hill, making a short cut, and come out some distance in advance of the others. The burdens carried by the camels were so great that one animal would often require the whole width of the road. They were bringing down dried fruits, peaches and apricots ; also green fruits, pomegranates and pineapples. The

common pottery and prayer-rugs used by the Mohammedans formed part of their burdens.

After the animals carrying the merchandise had
passed, came camels carrying the native women, for
many families were coming down to India to live. A
large dry-goods box was fastened to each side of the
camel, and in these the women were stored away, as
many as six or seven in a box. They belonged to
the high-caste people, so their faces were not allowed
to be seen, and their garments were so fashioned that
they covered the entire body. Two small holes were
cut out of the dress for the eyes, but aside from this
no feature of the women could be seen. Concealed
by this queer raiment the women were allowed to
come out of the zenanas and travel in the caravan.
The camels were driven by low-caste Afghan women,
who wore tattered trousers, and had wild-looking
eyes and screeching voices. They carried very heavy
sticks, with which they urged on a lazy camel or reminded an innocent-looking ass of their presence.

With these strange-looking people, and stranger
surroundings, I traveled back to India. At Pesha-
war, the English keep immense stacks of telegraph
poles and railroad ties and rails, that they may prepare for an outbreak at short notice, for Russia is
said to look with longing eyes in that direction. A
return to Lahore brought me to a place whence I
could reach almost any point in India by rail, and
from these central cities travel either by elephant or
camel to remote sections where native life could be
seen in all its varied forms.

Tomb at Lahore.

CHAPTER IV.

EACHING Central India I stopped off at Agra, the city noted for the most wonderful tomb ever erected in any part of the world —the Taj-Mahal. The traveler in India has the sight of this tomb ever before him through all his journeyings. It is to Hindustan what the volcano of Fusiyama is to Japan, and once seen, is never more to be forgotten. In the mind's picture gallery it remains chief of all that is artistic in the world. Strength of building has insured for four thousand years the preservation of the pyramids, but beauty alone has preserved this crowning glory of vast India.

The Great Mogul built the city of Agra; at his death his grandson, Shah Jehan, inherited his vast wealth and became a great spendthrift. Shah Jehan lived in Agra with his favorite wife, who bore him eight children and died at the birth of the ninth. When dying, his wife requested him to build a tomb to her memory that would surpass in splendor anything the world had ever seen. That he faithfully tried to carry out her request the Taj gives ample evidence. It was built two hundred and fifty years ago, and was twenty years in course of construction, twenty thousand men working on it daily. It cost several millions of dollars, which represent only the value of material, for the work was slave labor. The tomb is situated in a large garden on the banks of a softly flowing stream. It rests on a marble platform six feet high, is octagon in shape, built of pure white marble, with Arabic letters from the Koran mosaiced in black marble on the snow-white facings. The structure is surmounted by a large central dome and four smaller ones, one on each corner.

To see the Taj to advantage it must be viewed by moonlight. One night when the great city was wrapped in slumber we made our way, in company with a Christian guide, to the spot where the Taj stands. We passed under the great archway and along the winding path, amid playing fountains and blooming flowers, to the foot of the steps leading to the platform. A strange feeling took possession of me as I mounted those steps leading to a place of which I had read since childhood, but upon which I had never expected to look. We reached the platform and crossed to the door. Here my guide paused and lighted his small lantern; then we entered, to find ourselves in a good-sized room, a large portion of which was occupied by a finely-carved alabaster screen. The whole inside was finished with alabaster mosaiced with precious stones. Vines, flowers and buds were set in the wall, extending from floor to dome; the vines were of green stone, and the flowers and buds of jasper, amethyst, ruby, chrysolite and other valuable minerals. We passed through an archway in the screen, and sat on the marble stone

Tai-Mahal.

that marks the resting-place of the queen. My guide
said, "The most wonderful thing about the Taj is
the echo. Shall I sing something for you?" He
sang one verse of Coronation," two or three words
at a time. I heard the first words echoed from the
wall near the floor, rising higher and higher till they
reached the dome, where they were lost in the sweetest music. Wonderfully is one impressed with this
melodious echo. When all other sounds fade away
and are lost in the past, this seems ever and always
to abide with me.

It is thought by many that the women of India are
in a greatly improved condition under the British
control of the land. It is true that some little advance
has been made, but much more must be done before
the women of that country can ever be elevated to the
standard of womanhood. Some years ago, Pundita
Ramabai, a high-caste Indian, a widow, and daughter
of a Brahmin priest, became interested in the widows
of India, and never rested till she had established a
home for them. Ramabai is the most remarkable
woman that India has ever produced. Her father,
contrary to custom, believed in the education of women, whether wives or daughters. He educated his
wife and she assisted in the education of the daughter,
who felt she had a special mission to go from house
to house and arouse an interest in the education of
women. This prevented her marriage until the unusual age of sixteen, something almost unknown among
those people. She married a lawyer, but in little

more than a year and a half he died, leaving her branded for the rest of her life. She felt the sting of this so bitterly that her reason, her judgment, told her that there was something wrong in a system that branded a widowed woman and made her an object of contempt. She decided to go to Europe and see what the life of a woman in the Christian world was like. With her little girl, very young, she arrived in the great city of London, among people of whose tongue she knew nothing; but she learned the language, came to America, and raised a very large sum of money for her Widows' Home.

While in Powain I visited this fine institution, where I found forty-seven widows, some of them so small and young that it would be supposed that natural human kindness would have led to their protection; but they were despised, abused and even cast away, until the kind-hearted Ramabai gathered them in and cared for them.

Next to this remarkable woman, among those who have come out a benefactor to their people is Miss Soonderbai Powai, who has gone to England to plead with a Christian nation to come to the rescue of the people of India and deliver them from the withering, blighting curse of opium-smoking.

In crossing India I stopped at Jeypoor and visited the palace of the Rajah, who was very kind. He loaned me his elephant and a body-guard that I might visit the people of his domain. This was my first experience in traveling by elephant. The great ugly

Soonderbai Powai, Anti-Opium Agitator.

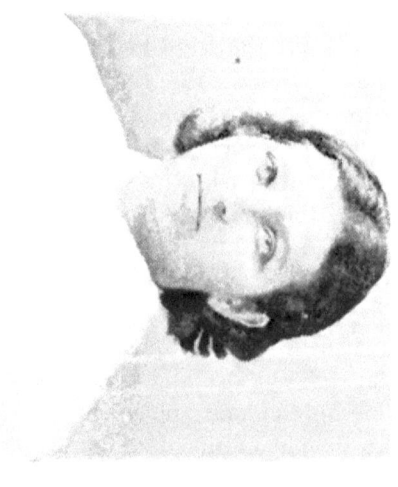

Pundita Ramabai, Friend of the Indian Widow.

creature got down with great effort on his knees and against his side was placed a ladder which had to be mounted to reach his back. With some difficulty, going two steps up and slipping back one, I reached the saddle, where I sat almost breathless till the guide and Bible-woman had mounted. The driver took his seat on the elephant's neck, just behind his ears, holding in his hand a long three-pronged fork, with which he pierced the poor creature mercilessly. The great beast rose slowly and started off with his burden, carrying us, day after day, over mountains, down into valleys, and through cities, with slow but sure tread, till I felt my worst experience in globe-trotting was surely not in viewing the landscape from the back of an elephant.

AFRICA.

CHAPTER I

KILLING TIME ON SHIPBOARD.

THE most cosmopolitan gathering in which I ever found myself was in a crowded steamer starting on a long voyage; better opportunity for studying character is rarely afforded. Is there anything in the world more interesting than the study of our fellow creatures, each cast in a different mold, with such varied characteristics? We look in wonder upon nature, studying it in all its forms, from the buttercup at our feet to the mighty oak lifting its proud head above us; we are fascinated by the skill of man, and stand amazed before his handiwork; but nothing affords such a source of never-ending study and surprise as humanity. The chance to indulge in such study came to me en route from Australia to Africa. It was in the month of May, the early autumn of the former land, that I took passage by the only line of steamers plying between those countries, and found myself among all conditions of men and women.

The voyage before us was long—one month out of sight of land. The steamer was a freight boat with passenger accommodations ; and even with delightful company the journey would not have been the most desirable thing to undertake. The day after we left, when all view of land was lost, we turned our attention to "getting settled." All were strangers to one another, and after a general summing up all round, and determining in our own minds who were the good-tempered and most companionable ones, we formed ourselves into little groups—to talk about the others. It was at the time of the great financial collapse in Australia. Many had lost all ; others, with what little remained, had turned their faces towards a new country, hoping in a brief time to retrieve their diminished estates. In Africa there was much excitement over recent discoveries of gold ; and thither most were journeying as toward the promised land. Many were hard-working people, who usually make up the population of mining regions the world over. Others were "speculators" — in plain English, gamblers. Two ladies were on their way to be married ; one had reached –yes, had passed—the midsummer of life, and amused herself by humming,

"This way I long have sought, and mourned because I found it not."

One couple were on their way to England to be married, taking their honeymoon in advance. Two doctors, intending to practice their arts on the unsuspecting miner, were among the number. An English millionaire, a young lady traveling alone, and a long, lean, lank individual, who proved to be delightful company, made up the passenger list.

The weather was stormy the first two weeks, and drove us under the awnings, where the limited space brought us together like a flock of sheep. These close relations proved to be not the most pleasant thing in the world, for we were sometimes forced to hear ourselves the subject of remark or criticism, a thing little calculated to add to the harmony of the trip. When the ancient spinster's joy over her happy estate was not the topic of discussion, the free ways of the younger were commented on. For the sake of excitement some of the party fell to match-making, and tried hard to break the monotony of the voyage by having a real wedding on board. This failed, so they decided to have a mock breach of promise trial; the engaged young lady sued a cross-eyed Jew for ten thousand pounds damaged affections, I being retained as her counsel. Of course the case was won.

When the storm was over and we once again sailed in calm waters, it was only to experience great discomfort in our cabins; for we were packed like sardines in a box, and the unventilated condition of the rooms inclined us to imagine that the "speculators" had gotten up "a corner" on air. One trying night, when life was a burden scarcely to be borne, and the heated condition of my cabin could no longer be endured, I threw my wrap about me and made my way to the deck. The lights were out, but I groped along to a bench, where I threw myself down, thinking to remain only a few moments. It was a dark, dark night; not even one star could be seen. Great sable clouds had rolled themselves up against the horizon like mountains of smoke, and only now and then could be seen the face of the moon passing through the rifts, to be almost instantly lost again in the blackness. Thus for a time it played hide-and-seek with the sea, upon whose bosom the reflected clouds seemed to spread themselves, till it, too, rolled in inky blackness about us.

Soon I heard the sound of voices near by, and became aware that I was not alone, though the hour was late. I lifted my head and peered into the darkness, straining my eyes in the direction whence the sound came. The clouds had again parted, and as the moon shone out for an instant I recognized two figures, who had now grown familiar to us, and of whom it was whispered, "They will make a match." I was evidently unobserved, so I resumed my reclining attitude and tried to sleep ; but my ears were too unaccustomed to the words that followed, for unintentionally I overheard this Romeo declare to his Juliet the tender passion that filled his heart. When he had exhausted all the adjectives at his command, and failed to express all that she was and ever could be to him, he paused, not so much to find words as to catch breath ; then with new strength and added vigor he "fell to" again, and finally concluded by gasping, as with his parting breath, "Oh, thou—oh, thou—." This was too much to longer endure. One may imagine the feeling of utter loneliness that would creep upon an old maid, away off in the middle of the sea on a dark night, in hearing such tender heart appeals and knowing that they were meant for another. I silently withdrew to meditate upon the strangeness of fate—perchance to slumber.

The captain was splendid company, and to the bridge I often betook myself to hear him, with great enthusiasm, tell of his efforts to solve the mysteries of the heavens. Standing with him one lovely night, when every star shone with a beauty wholly its own, the captain said, in a half-daring way, " Why don't you go to the mast-head ? " My reply was, " I will, if you will go with me." A gentleman on board, a special friend of the captain's, was to go with us. He was sent for, and our intention was told him, with strict injunctions " not to breathe a word about it "— but whoever knew or heard of a man keeping a secret? Before the appointed time it had been whispered among the passengers that a lady was going aloft that night. Great was the astonishment, and much the speculation as to who the lady was. About nine o'clock I withdrew to my cabin to prepare for this new experience. I drew forth the garment that always forms part of my wardrobe, a divided skirt— used only on special occasions—over which I put only a jacket that my feet might be perfectly free. I tied a scarf about my ears, for the night was chilly, and took a short cut, unobserved, to the bridge, where the gentlemen were in waiting.

From the bridge we crossed to the steerage quarters, where we mounted the rope at the side of the ship. My heart beat faster as I put my foot on the ladder and felt it give slightly ; but with the captain on one side and a fearless gentleman on the other, I took courage. "Look aloft," said the captain; and obeying his command, with face turned heavenward, I went up step by step till the end of the ladder was reached. It was my thought to set off a blue light, but the sails were all spread; at that height the wind was very strong, and with sparks flying into the rigging great damage might have been caused. It was a perfect night; the full moon shone in all its glory, throwing a flood of light upon the dancing waves as they went shimmering along in their wild unrest; and the stars twinkled their clear light upon us from the cloudless sky. From this height the people on the deck seemed like small children, as they nervously moved about awaiting our descent, which was more difficult than the climb upwards. I finally reached the deck in safety, amid the cheers of the passengers, and the "Well done; you are the first woman I have ever heard of who would venture to the mast-head," from the captain.

My last experience on the ship was the throwing overboard of a sealed bottle in which I had placed a note of greeting to the finder. This drifted thousands of miles, and was picked up some months later on the shores of a distant land by a gentleman, who at once notified me of his discovery.

With these varied incidents time wore away until we at last reached our desired haven.

CHAPTER II.

THE first sight of Africa was disappointing. It is true we saw Table Mountain, of which so much has been written, and to the summit of which almost every tourist wends his weary way, to return footsore and limping, but able to say, "I have been to the top of Table Mountain." It is about three thousand five hundred feet high, with a platform usually enveloped in a cloud of mist, which gives it the appearance of being spread with a white cloth—hence its name.

The first sight of Cape Town was also disappointing. I had expected to find a much larger city, with very different looking people. The natives appeared to be—and in fact are—a mixture of every race; they have intermarried until now they belong to no really distinct family, and are without distinguishing characteristics. They have partly adopted foreign dress and manners, and are the most uninteresting people I have ever seen. With the exception of a few old Dutch houses, the city is modern in appearance, and contains some fine buildings.

Like all other visitors, I, too, must go to the top of Table Mountain. Through the kindness of the mayor

it was arranged that I should reach the summit, and
at the same time save my strength and shoe leather.
On the top of the mountain a great reservoir was in
course of construction, and to carry material to the top
ærial cable lines had been put up. These consisted
of heavy wire ropes, extending from the apex of the
mountain to its foot ; an engine at each end kept the
cable in motion. Over these wires ran pulleys, to
which baskets were attached, and in one of these we
were to ascend three thousand five hundred feet.
The manager of the works and another gentleman
were to accompany me.

A long and delightful drive around the foot of the
mountain brought us to the side facing the sea, where
the engine house stands, from which point we were to
start. The perpendicular walls of the vast hill rose
before us, and the undertaking seemed most perilous.
We crowded ourselves into the basket, the signal was
given, and we moved slowly over the wire, suspended
in mid-air. I looked below, and saw the shadow grow
less and less till it seemed scarcely the size of my
hand. As we neared the face of the rock we hung at
rest for a few minutes until a workman gathered us
up, and we were landed on the top. There were a
fine view, wonderful works, and hundreds of men to
be seen ; and even a nice house—the home of the
manager—where we rested and partook of his hospitality. But, truth to tell, I was thinking about the
getting down again, and I confess I did not like the
idea, especially when the gentleman who was with us
said, "I would give anything if this trip were over."

When the time for the descent arrived, I walked to the edge of the summit, seated myself in the basket, and took courage for the down trip, which was accomplished in a few minutes; and then I, too, was able to say, "I have been to the top of Table Mountain."

Just out of Cape Town a few miles is one of General Booth's colonies. By kind invitation of the overseer I drove out to see what was being done to elevate a small portion of the "submerged tenth," in whose interests the General has so bravely worked. There is no doubt that if the poverty-stricken of the great cities could be brought to such places, and surrounded by similar influences, there would soon stand forth a mighty host for whose bettered condition they would forever bless General Booth. The colony in South Africa, if properly managed, will prove a great inspiration to many a weary pilgrim who has fallen in the struggle of life.

Very much has been said of the vexations of traveling in Africa; but the half was never told. In accordance with all that I had heard I equipped myself with spirit-lamp, teapot and tea, and such things as would add to the comfort of the journey, and boarded the train for Johannesburg, a city some twelve hundred miles distant. For a few hours we journeyed through a beautiful, well-cultivated country, but before the shadows of night had closed around us we came to a wild, weary waste, over which we were doomed to travel for two days and nights. This wilderness, which produces scarcely a blade of grass, is so vast in extent that even a field-

glass fails to reveal its limits. The wind, always
reduced to a low, sad wail, falls upon the ear like a
distant cry of distress, sweeps the desert the whole
journey through, and makes the nights almost
unbearable. We stopped only at a few small places,
to take coal or water ; but little of life—not even the
natives—is visible along the line. Those who see the
byways and highways of this great world of ours see
them at a terrible cost of bodily discomfort. At the
end of that long and tiresome journey I felt a fit subject for the hospital.

Johannesburg is a wonderful city ; I am almost
inclined to say worth the fatigue of the journey to see
it. The place is more than wonderful ; it stands out a
perfect marvel. Here is a city of forty-five thousand
people—a city containing some of the finest buildings
on the continent, erected at greater expense and labor
than that bestowed on any other modern town ; for
the rocks and stones from which the chief buildings
were reared were brought from a great distance, either
on mule-back or by bullock cart. Nothing but the
discovery of gold or diamonds could have gathered
together such numbers, or awakened such wide-spread
enthusiasm. In this case gold was the attraction, and
men became millionaires almost before they were
aware of it. It is the greatness of the place, rather
than its beauty, that so astonishes one. The immense
square in the center (which should be laid out as a
park) has been set aside for a market-place ; and here
each morning numbers of bullock carts, driven by
natives, bring wares to the city. The heavy wagons

are drawn by ten pairs of oxen, the first pair being
led by a native by means of a heavy strap. These
teams become so mixed that often much skill is
required in the separation.

Less than half an hour by rail is the city of Pretoria, the capital of the Transvaal. Between these
cities a deadly hatred seems to exist, doubtless because of the numbers of English who have come to
Johannesburg and made great fortunes. In their
enterprises they have greatly outdone the Boer, who
seems quite satisfied to follow in the footsteps of his
father and grandfather, and the very presence of the
English is regarded as an infringement on Dutch
rights.   .

At a large reception given by Sir Jacobus de Wit,
the English minister, I met the representatives of
France, Prussia, Germany, Belgium, the Hawaiian
Islands, and, in fact, those of all treaty countries.
The Belgian minister was a remarkable man, for
whom new regions had strong fascination. He was
possessed of a great desire to tread unknown parts—
"to step on sod never pressed by the foot of the
white man !" To this end he made preparation for an
extended trip to distant parts, taking with him several natives and camping out. After long days and
weary nights of travel he reached a lonely, forsaken
spot on a hillside, and there pitched his tent, believing he was far out of the track of his kind. A large
fire was kindled without the tent, and the lone min-
strel sat him down to pick the jews-harp. His soul
reveled in the delight that from that spot no white

face had ever looked into the starry firmament, no
eager soul had feasted on the wild beauty—this alone
was left for *him;* and with a satisfaction born of great
achievement he fell asleep.   The next morning he
betook himself to a cool seat under the long, feathery,
drooping limbs of a tropical tree to revel in solitude.
A native, following with a fur rug and a camp-stool
for the comfort of his master, found an empty sardine
box and a whisky bottle, which he tossed to one
side, and they fell almost at the feet of the Belgian.
The latter's disappointment was almost greater than
he could bear.   With uplifted eyes and extended
arms he exclaimed, "Great heaven! the Scotchman
has been here before me!"   Then turning in haste
from these "pioneers of civilization," he retraced his
steps, and for the future left unbeaten tracks for the
Scotchman.

By the kindness of the president of the Transvaal,
I was shown through the Mint, and thus my visits to
Pretoria and Johannesburg gave me an acquaintance
with the precious metal in all its stages, from the
rough ore to the burnished, small, flat pieces so much
coveted by the sons of men.   The scales on which the
finished money is tested are so delicately constructed
that they will correctly register the weight of a man
or a hair from his mustache.   A speck of dust will
throw them out of balance.   The Transvaal is full of
interest, but the people lack enterprise.   If Cecil
Rhodes had "right of way" in the republic, it would
soon be transformed, and, doubtless, the same developments would be brought about that have character-

A Scene in Africa.

ized his rule — for he rules—in Cape Colony. In
traveling southward along the east coast the modes of
conveyance discount the railway trains in real discomfort, and my courage almost failed me when I learned
that my next trip must be made in a ten-horse stage;
but later I had reason to congratulate myself that we
had the sure-footed horse instead of the fleet zebra
used in the north. The hour of starting was four in
the morning. Weary of flesh and sad of spirit I
dragged myself forth at the very hour when I was
wont to indulge in sweetest slumber, and mounted the
stage. The driver jumped lightly to the box, gathered up the reins, and before I knew it the mettlesome
steeds were speeding on their way.

The coach was filled with passengers, outside as
well as in. This gave it the appearance of being top-
heavy ; and as we swayed from side to side we were
in constant fear that those of us on the top would be
left by the wayside. The careless, almost reckless,
manner of the driver was in no way calculated to
inspire confidence, and my only thought was, "How
awful it will be when night comes on."

Night came. The rocking, rolling and shaking
continued with unabated fury till the small hours of
the morning, when we stopped for refreshments and
a few hours' rest—our misery to begin again at dawn.
The following day the stewing, broiling and semi-
congealing—according to the various states of the
temperature—came to an end, and we arrived in
safety at the east coast. This section of the country
was wholly unlike that through which I had just

fought my way ; the heavy winds of the Karroo, which seem to be on contract (as is everything else in Africa) to blow just so much in a given space, had been left behind, and from the surrounding beauty it was difficult to realize that we were not in some other part of the world. The barren wastes of the desert had given way to tropical foliage ; and the moaning wind was lost in the fresh sea air that blew softly over the land, subduing the clouds of dust that until then had continuously enveloped us.

Continuing the journey southward we came to Queenstown, where we saw the first real native village, some two or three miles from the city. This was inhabited by Kaffirs, who received us with great hospitality, showing us through their houses, and giving us any desired information. The Kaffirs are of a somewhat lower order of intellect than that I had expected to find ; and to educate and evangelize them is, in my opinion, an almost hopeless task, though the missionaries report great progress in this direction.

In these parts the natives are not so black as are the negroes of the United States, but they are much less intellectual in appearance. The men wear only a blanket wrapped around them ; no matter how hot the sun, or cold the wind, this ever abides with them. In some way these blankets are dyed a deep terra-cotta color, and one blanket serves the wearer for years. From appearance, I should say some of them had been handed down for several generations.

The men are lazy, and their highest ambition is to possess themselves of a certain number of cattle ;

with these they are able to purchase a number of
wives. In increasing his wives the Kaffir increases
his stock in trade, for the women perform all the hard
labor. When a man is the happy possessor of three
or four wives, it means support and laziness for the
rest of his life. He places the same value on a wife
that he would on any live stock.

Kaffir villages and houses are built in circular form,
for the Kaffir mind is wholly unequal to forming a
square, just as a circle is beyond the skill of a Hottentot. A large open space is selected, and the huts are
built near one another, and then inclosed by a stone or
earth wall. The huts are most curiously constructed.
Limber poles are set in the ground in circular form,
about three feet apart. When these are all placed,
the ends are brought together at the top and fastened. This forms the framework of the house, making it cone shape; it is then interwoven with heavy
waterproof grass. The entire frame is covered, leaving only space for a low door, to enter which one must
almost crawl—or at least bend very low. The huts
are without chimneys or windows, and are wholly destitute of furniture. The floor serves for a bed; and
the natives sleep in the same blanket worn in the
day. Thus their wants are very few. The fire is
kindled on the floor, and as there is no outlet for
smoke, everything is heavy with the odor of burnt
wood or grass. The occupants of these huts subsist
chiefly on a kind of corn, which is eaten with a great
spoon from the vessel in which it is cooked.

The Kaffir women are low of stature, and wear two

blankets instead of one, both of which are of the same hideous color. One is tied around the waist ; the other is thrown over the shoulders in cool weather, but is cast off during the hot season, when the upper part of the body is without cover. Some of the women are very shapely, and, unlike the men, many have fine features, which are often disfigured, however, by an ugly paint of the color of the blankets. Like all natives they are fond of showy ornaments, and bedeck themselves with beads of every color on the arms to the elbows, and around the neck, extending to the waist. They usually build the houses, perform most of the heavy labor, and occupy the same place that woman has always held in the heathen countries of the world.

CHAPTER III.

EACH country and age has its heroes, martyrs and geniuses. In every land the halo of greatness rests upon some brow whose reflected light shines across the seas to other lands bearing on its shimmering beams a name that becomes an inspiration to the world. The thought of "darkest" has been so long associated with the name of Africa that one would scarcely expect to discover anything which could be designated by the name of "genius," yet it is a fact that from that dark land there have been flashed over the wires of the world names whose greatness has left its imprint upon our day.

While traveling through this country, in many respects so uninteresting, I met men and women who had distinguished themselves, and whose names were enrolled upon the book of fame. I suppose the best known woman in Africa is Olive Schreiner, or, perhaps, I should say the best known family is the Schreiner family, of which Olive is the most distinguished. It is not an exceptional thing to find one member of a family who possesses gifts beyond the usual; but to find a whole family of geniuses, with gifts so varied that they compass the entire range of modern thought, is something indeed extraordinary. Yet each one of the Schreiner family stands out a character by itself. Olive was introduced to the literary world under the somewhat singular name of "Ralph Iron," and through the medium of a book which was a decided departure from the usual line of thought—"The Story of an African Farm." I read the book soon after it appeared in America, and because of its peculiar theology and remarkable views concerning the marriage question—which had not then been developed into a "question," but was accepted, as it had been handed down to us, as a divine institution, and therefore the only form that could be recognized—because of these strange ideas I had a great desire to see the writer. When the success of the book was assured and the real name of its author had become known, I was filled with a greater desire than ever to look into the face of the woman who had penned this somewhat weird production. The opportunity came to me during my sojourn in Africa when I visited Olive Schreiner in her home.

Her book being without a frontispiece of the writer, the only idea to be formed of her personal appearance must of necessity be based on the characteristics of the book. These being so unusual, it was but natural to expect to see a somewhat unusual appearing individual. With these thoughts in my mind I left the train at a station a short distance from Craddock, and found the carriage waiting to convey me to the farm, some three miles distant.

Olive Schreiner.

Viewing the surrounding country as we drove along, I did not see how any place in that region could be called a farm. My whole being just tingled with suppressed interrogation-points, as I wondered what such barren land could produce. Arrived at the farm, a little body flitted from the house to the gate to welcome me, and in less than five minutes I was truly at home with this interesting, chatty little woman.

Mrs. Schreiner is under average height, with dark hair, arranged in that careless style so becoming to genius. Her dark, sparkling eyes light up her face with wonderful brightness as she expresses the interest she feels in all things; for, from this place where one seems almost buried, she keeps in perfect touch with the outside world and its "doings." This kind of life, that would narrow down and dwarf the very soul of some women, is to her a perpetual feast.

The house is of the style of the farm-houses of that country—comfortable, but scarcely presenting the surroundings in which one would expect to find Olive Schreiner. It is impossible at such distant points to procure the furnishings and belongings of the kind of house that charms and quiets the untamed spirit of a restless woman. Every real need was supplied, and for actual comfort nothing was wanting, but there were none of the luxuries present that characterize the modern household. This was one of the penalties of living in the "wilds of Africa," for such this great farm—with ten thousand acres—seemed. On one hand the high, barren, ugly hills, which form one

of the fascinations of the place for Mrs. Schreiner,
shut out the view. On the other, is Fish river, usually dry. Beyond this stretches the great "karroo,"
wild, vast and awful, over which the wind sighs like
a symbol of endless sorrow. For months at a time
the whole landscape is parched and burned, with little
signs of vegetation ; when finally this does appear,
the low bushes are almost the color of the earth from
which they spring—a strange gray-green that lends,
if possible, a more barren aspect to the country.

As we stood in the door of her house, Mrs.
Schreiner pointed toward the hills with great enthusiasm, told of the animals that prowl among the
bushes, and seemed to revel in the beauty (?) of a
landscape that to me breathed only of endless waste.
She was, if anything, even more enthusiastic in her
delight in the great "karroo."

"I just love it," said she, "for its mighty vastness. I am filled with awe when I look upon its
almost boundless stretches, spreading over miles of
uninhabited regions. I have almost a reverence for
it." Then, pointing in the direction which we then
faced, she added, "Away over there, in a small
house, I wrote my story of 'An African Farm'; it
was the majesty of the almost limitless 'karroo' that
gave me my inspiration."

I did not discuss the theology or social features of
the book, which I fully intended to do, for she talked
on about the country and of things generally in
which she is so well informed, that time wore apace,
and I was obliged to depart without having gained

Fish River, Schreiner Farm.

the information whether or not the book expressed her own personal views. Later I was told that she was but nineteen years of age when this remarkable production was brought out. It is said that from her publishers she received the small amount of fourteen pounds, to which, however, they added large sums when the book proved such an astonishing success.

The next in interest was " Olive Schreiner's hus-band," as he is generally called in South Africa. Mr. Schreiner, previous to his marriage with Olive, was a Mr. Conwright ; but finding his wife unwilling to give up a name that had become known through-out the world, he took hers ; a proceeding made easy in that country by simply announcing in the papers for a certain time that after such a date Mr. John Smith will be known as Mr. John Smith Brown, or Green, as the case may be. Numerous criticisms have been passed pro and con on his unusual course, and I venture to say that sentiment generally is much against a man "losing his identity in his wife's name," as a number have expressed it. However, I found Mr. Schreiner just the sort of a man one would expect Olive Schreiner to marry, and it was most amusing to hear her tell, in her bright, spark-ling way, how they became engaged—sometimes hav-ing a good-natured laugh at her husband's expense.

Mr. Schreiner is a man of fine appearance, some-what older than his wife, and, it is said by those who should know, one of the rising statesmen of South Africa. Being indigenous to the country (he has never been out of it), he is deeply interested in all

social and political questions, and especially those per-
taining to the welfare of the natives, for whom he expressed a great fondness. His power as a writer on
local subjects, and his unusual platform ability, will
doubtless place him where both gifts will tell in the
interests of the people. Previous to his marriage,
Mr. Schreiner lived a bachelor life on his farm for
some years. During this time he gathered about him
a large number of native servants, both Hottentots
and Kaffirs. These became servants indeed, for it is
not overstating it to say that many of them would
have given their lives for him, if necessary. When I
was there the Schreiners were about to leave the farm,
and Mr. Schreiner's greatest grief seemed to be that
he must part with his servants. The place is very
extensive, and is principally a stock farm ; that is, if
the ostrich can be classified under the head of stock.
Over this wild-looking place some hundreds of these
birds of the desert roam at large, and scarcely know
that a barbed wire fence keeps them within its con-
fines.

CHAPTER IV.

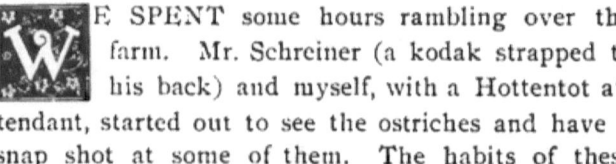E SPENT some hours rambling over the farm. Mr. Schreiner (a kodak strapped to his back) and myself, with a Hottentot attendant, started out to see the ostriches and have a snap shot at some of them. The habits of these ungainly birds are most interesting. They can never be tamed, and it is very dangerous to go within reach of the ugly feet and legs that possess so much strength. As we approached the breeding-yards the birds took flight at the appearance of a stranger, and started on a wild run, in which even a horse could not have overtaken them, so fleet of movement were they. Nature has provided them with special means of swiftness in the tail and wing feathers, and as they increase their speed these are spread like small sails, presenting an amusing appearance. The movement of their legs is wholly lost sight of, and they have the appearance of skimming along without effort. The birds when enraged are savage and dangerous, and a more blood-curdling sight could not be witnessed than that of an encounter with these vicious creatures.

With the aid of the Hottentot, Mr. Schreiner caught an old bird and held it while I plucked a few feathers. The poor thing kicked, struggled and floundered around, and when liberated soon put good distance between us. The hen bird is most savage when sitting, and if disturbed gives fair warning to the intruder. In some marvelous manner the long neck, which can be lengthened to some feet, is drawn down to the body and only the head appears from amid a frill of feathers that fairly stand on end. To give vent to her displeasure she opens wide her mouth, and thunders forth her rage in volumes of sound that fall upon the ear like the roaring of a wild bull. It is wonderful, the special gifts that nature has bestowed upon the female portion of all creation—they can at least make a noise. On the principle of "equal division of labor," both birds sit in turn to bring out the young.

In strolling about I came upon a nest of eggs, and saw how the sand had been scratched to make a hollow in which to deposit the great white balls that later on would be transformed into life. The gray bird, which is the female, has less plumage than the male, and sits in the day ; being the same color as the grass in which her nest is made, she remains unseen, and as the day grows old the male bird, whose color mingles with the surrounding darkness, hovers over the eggs until returning light. When the ostriches are partly grown they are at their ugliest stage. Numbers are placed in a small inclosure, the walls just high enough to keep them within ; at the slightest sound they poke their long necks over the wall, perhaps fifty in a row, with no part of their

Discovering a Nest of Ostrich Eggs.

bodies in sight, but a yard or two of neck bobbing up and down as they try to take in the situation. According to modern methods most of the chicks are brought out in an incubator.

To the hatching-room we proceeded to inspect the process of eggs "evoluting" into chicks. The eggs were deposited in long drawers, and uniform heat was maintained by the aid of a lamp. "In this drawer," said Mr. Schreiner, as he pulled out the one nearest the floor, "they must be almost ready to come out." Sure enough, there they were struggling with a heavy shell, trying to clear themselves of the bits that seemed to cling so fondly to these little ugly creatures. One, with more determination than the rest, stood up, shook the few fragments of shell from his down, and started off with the independence of a Yankee going to celebrate the Fourth of July. In this early stage of life they seem all head and feet, their two great, ugly toes being the most prominent feature. The breast is a pretty fawn color, but the back is covered with quills which turn the wrong way, very similar to porcupine quills when raised. When removed from place to place they are carried by the neck, which seems most cruel, but in no way injures them. When grown the birds are plucked every eight months. Many have written at length of the cruelty of plucking the ostrich, and some humane and well-disposed persons have passed resolutions and pledged themselves not to wear the plumage when, as a matter of fact, the birds suffer no more than we would in having our hair cut. They are herded into a pen, a sack is placed over their heads, and the plumes are cut off, leaving the stumps of the quills on the body. These are shed in molting season, just as the feathers would be if allowed to remain. The eggs are of great size, and the weight surprising. The shell, when opened and the inside removed, will hold the contents of eighteen hen eggs. Ostrich eggs are sometimes used for table purposes ; they are usually made into omelets, one egg being sufficient for a meal for a whole family. Having a desire to sample this ovicular delicacy to see what it might be like, Mrs. Schreiner boiled one for sandwiches to be taken on my journey ; she put it on to cook in the morning, and when it had boiled for nearly an hour it was considered well done.

Mrs. Schreiner is not especially fond of the ostrich, but the hundreds of Cashmere goats and Persian sheep on the farm have in her a true friend. I have rarely seen a prettier sight than this happy husband and wife counting the goats when they come home at night. They are valuable for their long, pretty silk wool, which hangs almost to the ground. The sheep are raised for the table and market. Of the goats there were a large number. The native shepherds brought them from the hillsides where they had been feeding during the day, and they all huddled together near the gate of the inclosure where they were to spend the night. Mr. Schreiner stepped over the fence, opened the gate, and the goats began to file in, as if each understood that he must not enter until the one before him had been counted. The Persian sheep

A Hottentot Hut.

are kept separate. They are most peculiar in appearance, with long, white bodies, closely clipped wool and black heads. They scramble, uncounted, into their place of shelter, and little interest is taken in them.

Some have asked, "What will be the effect of Olive Schreiner's marriage; will her genius and identity be lost in that of her husband?" No, I should say not. She will always be Olive Schreiner. Her individuality is too marked and strong to be lost in anyone. The same elements that gave her the courage to dip her pen in a new color of ink, as it were, and give her convictions to the world—which were only new in so far that she was brave enough to write them—these elements will always maintain for her a striking personality; and Mr. Schreiner is himself so strong a character that he has no need of his wife's personality to add to his strength.

Another question often asked is, "What about her husband taking her name?" In these days when there is divided opinion on all points that pertain to the "doings" of women, this question will be answered according to the "evoluted" thought of the inquirer. From the expressions of opinion I gathered while in that country, I should say that Mr. Schreiner's example would be somewhat disastrous to the general "run" of men; but Mr. Schreiner, happily, is a man strong enough to carry his wife's name. All men are not. The weight would carry some down to oblivion, or if they lived at all it would be in the reflected light from a woman, which always casts a rather sickly irradiation upon a man. The conviction grows upon me that the less pronounced gifted women can be in winning their way to the sure footing intended for them by nature and God, the more rapid will be their progress toward that goal.

My visit to this home will ever be remembered with delight.

CHAPTER V.

AS DAY was slowly dying from the sky we drove to the railway station, some few miles distant, and I boarded the train going southward, intending to visit the town where Mrs. Schreiner's mother has so long lived. The train was cold, and great was my discomfort. Through the dark, moonless night I waited for the dawn, which would bring me beyond these plains where the wind sighed like the restless ocean upon the shore.

Morning found me in a small city by the sea, nestled at the foot of the hills. The weird desert was far behind ; the damp air and the mists from the sea had been distilled into dew, which watered the parched earth and dried roots, giving new life to all around.

I had come to this place especially to see Olive Schreiner's mother, of whom her daughter had spoken much. "My mother," she had said, "has been converted to the Roman faith, and you will find her in the convent."

Toward the convent I set my face, and reached the great iron gates and high walls just as the day pupils were leaving school. Following the directions given,

I soon reached the house in which lives one of the most remarkable women of her age I have ever known. The door was opened by Mrs. Schreiner herself, and I found it almost impossible to believe that eighty-seven years had swept over her head. I was ushered into a room, the walls of which were completely covered with pictures, most of them relating to her religious faith. The house is small, for she lives alone and is very active. Her domestic duties are but a recreation to her. A look into her face told me where Olive had got her bright eyes, that are such a charm, and a few moments' conversation told me through whom Mother Nature had bestowed such marvelous conversational powers upon Olive Schreiner. For fourteen years Mrs. Schreiner has lived alone, and twice only has ventured beyond the great gates in that time. I was surprised, finding her so shut away, to learn how thoroughly she was informed on matters of interest in the outside world; but she "keeps up with the times" through the medium of all kinds of papers and periodicals. Being deeply interested in all good work, she spends much time in prayer for the success of old reforms. In motherly tones she said:

"Yes, child, I remember well when you started on your mission, and thought you young to go out into the great cruel world from which I was so glad to be sheltered."

Knowing the religious views of other members of her family, I wanted much to learn how she became a Roman Catholic; so I ventured to say:

" Mrs. Schreiner, do you mind telling me how you became interested in the Roman faith ? "

" No, I don't mind in the least."

Then I drew forth my ever-present note-book and recorded most of what she said.

" My husband," began Mrs. Schreiner, " was a Dutch missionary greatly devoted to his work, and deeply interested in the natives.   During our married life three sons and two daughters were given us—my son in England ; the one in the government ; Theo., the temperance lecturer ; Mrs. Lewis, who has not long been married ; and my Olive.   All these are living and are children of whom I am proud—not a black sheep among them."

The sweet gratitude with which she expressed this fact was delightful to see, for with the sun of her last days flooding her path, truly it must be a blessing to look upon a family of men and women grown, and see them filling places of honor in the world.

" Well," continued she, " my husband died, the children were away, and I broke up the home and went to live with a friend."   Here, with moistened eyes and a trembling in her voice, she spoke feelingly upon the sacred theme of friendship.

" In that hour of sorrow, when the husband of all these years had gone before me and left me with a longing heart and empty life, the refuge of a sweet friendship was in a great measure a compensation. To this friend I confided everything.   There was not an act of my life, thought of my heart, or longing of my soul that I did not tell her.   We were knit to-

gether as were the souls of David and Jonathan.
When a friend is wound and bound about the heart
till the fibers of one life can scarcely be separated
from those of the other, and in each there seems a
consciousness of the absolute need of the other, that
happy state is as near bliss as we shall arrive in this
world. Often and often I have blessed heaven for
the sweetness of a pure friendship. But when the
loss of my husband seemed most severe, there came
the darkest hour of my life ; my friend proved un-
faithful, and in one day I was robbed of what was
more than life to me. Sad of heart and heavy of
spirit, I lost faith in man and God. I believed in
nothing, and life had little charm for me. In this
frame of mind I accepted an invitation to spend a few
days with a friend whom I had long known. Glad to
escape from the heart-burnings that made life a burden, I went to spend Christmas-tide with her. My
friend belonged to the Catholic faith, and without
knowing my frame of mind she invited me to the
Christmas service. The sweet music attracted me,
and I went from time to time, until I became interested in the faith of the church. The priest visited
me often ; I studied the Bible, and was at last
brought to light through the teaching of the
Roman Catholic church.''

Here she looked me in the face, and with an intense earnestness said, '' And, child, I have found
the true religion. These are the happiest days of
my whole life.'' She spoke with tender affection of
the religious belief of her children and concluded by

saying, "That, perhaps, is the religion for them, but this is the religion for me."

There was something sweetly pathetic about the life of this devoted woman, who at her advanced age retains all her faculties and a full interest in the world and, most surprising of all, picks up a newspaper of ordinary print and reads it off without glasses. Mrs. Schreiner asks nothing greater than that she may live and die in the faith to which she is so strongly attached.

CHAPTER VI.

N undertaking a journey of long distance, the fatigue was so great that I stopped off at a small town to rest for the night. In the local papers I read that Mr. Theo. Schreiner, who had been holding wonderful temperance meetings at a point near by, would reach town the following morning. Here was an unexpected opportunity to meet another member of the family of whom I had heard so much. My departure was delayed to await his arrival. When his card was sent up I went down to meet him, full of expectation as to what this particular Mr. Schreiner might be like. As I entered, he rose and greeted me in a warm, friendly way. We had each read much of the other, and we felt that we were by no means strangers. There stood before me a fine-looking man, who bore little resemblance to his sister Olive. About the average height, with thick light hair, and beard to match, and large blue eyes, he certainly looked a splendid specimen of an Africana. Mr. Schreiner's special gift lies in his unusual platform ability. He is considered one of the finest speakers in the country. He has utilized his gift of eloquence in the interest of reform, and for many many years has gone up and down the land, among the Boers, speaking on all subjects for the betterment of the people. He can discourse in Dutch like a Hollander, and his special theme is gospel temperance.

When I was about to start for the station, he proposed that we go early enough to drive around the town. It was a small place, and very little time would suffice to see the "sights." The object of greatest interest was a monument, the like of which the world has never seen. It is usually supposed that monuments stand to do honor to the valiant deeds of some great hero, but this was by no means the object of the granite column that arrested my attention as we drove along. Some time ago it was decided that the English tongue should be the language of Parliament; no one would be eligible for Parliament who did not speak both English and Dutch, but English was to be the recognized language. This was greatly lamented by the Boer, who vainly supposed his language to be that of heaven. It is never defamed by using its strongest adjectives; hence a Boer reads his Bible and prays in high Dutch, but does all his swearing in low Dutch. Believing it to be the language used in calling the world into being, and having a reverence for it second only to that for the Most High, it was a great grief to see it crushed to earth with one fell swoop, and know that its musical accents would no longer enter into the laws of the land. This event, therefore, called forth the patriotism of the Boer, who expressed it by the erection of this monument.

"Would you like to read the inscriptions?" asked

Mr. Schreiner. Being a Yankee, I felt I could invest my time to greater profit even in Africa then sitting down to decipher the hieroglyphics on a tombstone put up to a dead language ; so we drove on to meet the train.

Some days later, my line of travel took me to Kimberley, the home of Mrs. Staksby Lewis, the oldest sister of Olive Schreiner, and wholly unlike her in every possible way. Low of stature and very stout, with a somewhat strained voice from long public speaking, she had the appearance of a home-body instead of a platform woman. Long ago Mrs. Lewis associated herself with temperance reform, and devoted her unbounded energies to the Good Templars, who are still wont to call her "Sister Schreiner," notwithstanding her little flock of nine, none of whom belong to her, however.

Upon the death of a relative, or friend, I do not recollect which, Mrs. Lewis (then Miss Schreiner) adopted four children. As she went from place to place speaking, sometimes many consecutive nights, "her children" were always with her, and, in addition to her public duties, she seemed to find time to instruct and train them. During her travels Miss Schreiner met Mr. Staksby Lewis, a widower with five children, most of whom were well grown. For some years she considered his proposal of marriage ; finally, it seemed to be the call of duty, and she settled down to the domestic cares that come to a woman who undertakes to mother nine children of two different families, none of them her own.

Mr. Lewis is a friendly, quiet man of sterling worth, and wholly devoted to his wife and family. Mrs. Lewis is of an intense religious nature, her special belief being "faith healing," a doctrine to the study of which she has devoted much time. The earnestness of her platform utterances has won many converts to that live train of thought.

Of the Schreiner family there remain only two— brothers—of whom I have not spoken. One has long been associated with the government of South Africa, and the other took up his residence in England some time ago where he leads a less public life.

ORIENTAL OBSEQUIES.

CHAPTER I.

A JAPANESE FUNERAL.

HE ordinary individual is destined to attract attention at least twice, and often thrice, before he forever disappears from the active scenes of this world. The most important event of life, one's birth, calls forth less interest than the two events which follow—the wedding and the funeral. For the latter greater preparations are generally made and a more wide-spread interest is taken. When the wee babe first opens its eyes and the announcement goes forth, " Unto us a son is born," or "a daughter is given," the fact is quietly recorded and usually forgotten by all beyond the sound of the voice of the new-comer. But when a wedding is on the boards, interest deepens, whole neighborhoods and even cities become awakened, and crowds gather to see "what the bride's dress is like"; and thus, amid the vulgar stare of the throng, a sweet, blushing maiden becomes the object of curiosity, criticism and comment. To my mind it is far worse than are some of the customs we are wont to call " heathen." When the wedding is over, and, finally, the lengthened or shortened thread of life is broken, the funeral attracts the crowds; many who never spoke a kindly word of the dead bring forth their garlands fair to deck the coffin, or to wilt and fade upon the grave; and in the dying of their fragrance and beauty they carry with them, perhaps, the last thought of the one gone before.

In studying the customs of the people of the world, I was deeply interested in comparing the funeral and wedding ceremonies of Asia with those of Christian lands; but it is of funerals only that I can here find time to speak. As the customs vary so greatly, it would be impossible to describe them all ; it is there-fore necessary to confine myself to the extent of my own observations.

Soon after landing in the city of Yokohama, Japan, I was told that a wealthy and noted native had died, and his funeral would take place the following Sun-day in one of the great temples. As we went out into the streets on that day, it was an easy matter to find the place of the obsequies by following the crowds, for the streets were teeming with people, all flocking to honor the dead. After a long walk we reached the avenue that led to the temple, which stood at the top of the street. The roads to the right and to the left were thronged with some fifty thou-sand people. The short avenue in front of the temple was kept clear for the funeral procession. As a spe-cial favor I was allowed to walk down the avenue ; otherwise I would have been unable to reach the temple, for the crowds were so great. The whole street was lined with floral decorations, in which the Japanese greatly excel. Large trees, planted in tubs, were placed a few feet on each side, and extended from the beginning of the avenue to the very temple door. Many kinds of flowers were arranged in the branches of these trees to give them the appearance of blooming shrubs. We were escorted up the walk by two native policemen ; reaching the temple we found a heavy rope stretched across the great steps to keep the crowds back. The policemen explained that we were strangers and anxious to go into the service, and the guards kindly allowed us to enter.

The temple was constructed after the manner of the architecture of that country, with an open front, so that all proceedings could be witnessed from the street. The usual lack of order and solemnity prevailed; for nowhere in the east can be found decorum at worship, funerals, weddings or other functions which we regard as sacred and carry on with more or less system. At one side stood the coffin, which was in the form of a miniature temple, resting on a bier. This small temple was made of some kind of white spruce, beautifully carved, but without polish or finish. The pointed eaves extended over the sides, and beneath them were small carved windows, draped with white lace curtains and lined with pale blue. The whole "casket" had more or less carved open work upon it. Near the coffin stood a band of musicians dressed in foreign uniform. They wore dark blue trousers, red coats, and played on foreign instruments. On the

other side of the room stood the relatives and inti-
mate friends, distributing presents; this is a general
custom among the wealthy or upper classes. The
presents usually consist of sweets made from rice
flour and sugar, and fashioned after the lotus blossom
and leaf. In the center of the room sat numbers of
priests clothed in black gauze, reading or chanting a
sort of dirge from their sacred book, the music of the
band almost drowning the monotony of their voices.

When this confusing ceremony came to a close the
funeral procession formed. I had no idea who the
mourners were, for none were weeping or wailing or
clad in any kind of mourning-garb; all were chatting
away, each seeming to express an opinion as to how
the proceedings should be carried on. The coolies,
bearing the coffin, were dressed in white garments
with a white, drooping head covering. The place of
burial was some distance off, and numbers of these
coolies formed relays to relieve each other at stated
intervals. Those not in service at the moment preceded the remains, and, behind, came the pall-bearers.
Numbers of ordinary coolies bore the trees and tubs,
taking them, as they passed, from the sides of the
streets, and with them a great throng moved on to
the burial-ground. The distance was too great to
follow. I was told no special service was held at the
grave; the remains were interred in the most simple
way.

Just across the small body of water that separates
two nations, I found a great difference in the manners
and customs of the people.

CHAPTER II.

FIRST witnessed a Chinese funeral in the streets of Victoria, on the island of Hong Kong. As I passed along a strange noise attracted my attention, and looking in the direction whence it came I saw a large moving crowd, and resolved to see what it might mean. I retreated from the street to the steps of a native shop, and there awaited the advancing throng, which proved to be a Chinese funeral. A long procession, made up of strange-looking people, was headed by small boys carrying wooden signs, or banners. These were inscribed with those fiendish hieroglyphics, with innumerable horns and hoofs, that give one the impression that the language is of a warmer climate than that of China. These banners were carried far above the heads of the bearers, and the inscriptions were supposed to recount the virtues of the dead. Following the mourners, wailers filed in line, for this was the funeral of a well-to-do person. Numbers were hired to wail and cry ; ten or a dozen were dressed in white, with cone-shaped covers made of white calico on their heads ; these covers drooped far over the face, completely concealing the features. The mourners formed in procession, single file, headed by one who continu-

ally tooted a tin horn. This personage was followed
by one who lent support to the chief mourner. As
they marched they swayed their bodies to and fro,
and howled, and moaned, and sobbed ; the one who
made the most noise was accounted the best mourner,
and probably received the largest amount for his
services. Behind the mourners the pall-bearers slowly
marched, as if trying to keep step with the loud
wails. The coffin was large, and looked heavy. It
was flat on the bottom, oval at the sides, with a
curved lid, and a heavy piece extending upward from
one end, which marked the head, for it was the same
width all the way down. Large ropes were bound
about it and the ends were made fast to a piece of
bamboo, which was placed over the shoulders of the
men, leaving the coffin to wobble about as they
marched along.

The thought of a bier has never occurred to these
people, for it is not in the nature of a Chinaman to
devise labor-saving methods. Behind the coffin followed bearers of sweets and meats to be placed on
the grave of the departed and consumed at his leisure. A pyramid-shaped tier of shelves were ladened
with food of all kinds, including a whole roast pig,·
fowls, ducks, and many savory bits seldom tasted
in the life of an ordinary Chinaman. The running
and hurrying of some parts of the procession as they
occasionally became detached from the other by reason of the large crowds, the endless din of the noise
they called ''music,'' mingled with the sound of

wailing voices, made a scene of confusion not easily described and never to be forgotten.

The selection of a place of burial is the chief concern of the relatives, for much of the future state of happiness depends upon where the bones of the departed rest. Frequently days elapse before an auspicious spot –away from the range of the wind which blows "bad luck,"—can be settled on. When a "safe" spot has been found, the coffin is placed on the ground, and a mound of earth thrown over it; this often reaches the height of six feet. The place is forever sacred, and must on no account be disturbed. Frequently the graves are marked by cutting the slope from one side of the mound and building in some kind of masonry. At certain times of the year paper money is burned before the grave, for the benefit of the dead. This, however, cannot be said to be the usual custom of disposing of the dead, for in each of the forty-two provinces the natives have their several superstitions and forms.

In one of the northern cities I saw a funeral among the lower classes. The coffin was carried in the manner described, but there was no procession beyond the relatives, and no extra mourners. The coffin had passed before I caught sight of it, but my attention was arrested by a number of weeping persons riding on wheelbarrows. I called a coolie and followed up the procession of six wheelbarrows, on which were seated nine weeping women and three men. It never dawned upon me that it might be a funeral. Wheelbarrow travel, which is the usual mode in these

parts, was unique, and the thought of being wheeled
to a funeral in one of those unsightly conveyances
overcame the solemnity that the occasion demanded,
and I confess I overtook that funeral procession in
a frame of mind unfit to offer my services as one
of the hired wailers. The mourners were chiefly
women, and, being of the poorer class, could not
afford the expense of white garments for mourning
apparel ; so their grief was indicated by a strip of
white muslin bound about the head, with the ends
left dangling down. The grief they failed to express by way of garb was made up in noise, as
they threw themselves from side to side, with many
hairbreadth escapes from landing in the road. Thus
they made their way to the burying-ground without
their noisy demonstrations of grief attracting the
least attention from the passer-by—for the scene is a
common one.

In a town somewhat inland I met with a greater
surprise than that afforded by the wheelbarrow procession. It was in a small village, where a foreigner
attracted much attention, and my presence in the town
brought out a great following as I went from house to
house speaking to the women. In one small house
the woman invited me in, more, I think, to see what
I was like than to hear what I had to say. As I sat
perched upon a saw-horse, a common seat among the
poor, I saw a very rude coffin against the wall on the
opposite side of the room. When the crowds of men
and women pushed in, several seated themselves upon
the coffin, and almost sat upon each other as they

Burning the Dead in India.

tried to make room for one more. The thought came to me that probably they had purchased it at "a bargain," and were keeping it in readiness, thinking, at the same time, that it would serve as a warning of our "common end"; but it was only my Yankee proclivities that led me to such conjectures. It was the custom in those parts whenever the husband or the wife died, to embalm the remains and keep the coffin in the house until the death of the other, and, finally, bury them together. The husband of this family had been dead seven years, and the coffin had been in the house all the time!

Before leaving the town I returned to say a last word to the woman, thank her for her kindness, and leave a copy of the Bible in her language. I did not enter, but stood in the doorway a sufficient time to make mental notes of the scene before me. On the coffin sat a young child eating rice from a bowl with its hands. An old hen and her brood of chicks had come into the house (a way they have in that country), and, being on familiar terms with the child, had hopped up on the coffin and helped herself to a mouthful of rice, which she threw to the floor in small particles, and, in hen language, called the little ones to partake of the feast. The child was willing to share the rice with this wise fowl, and seemed rather pleased at the familiar relations existing between them. Considering the many uses to which these coffins are put, perhaps the custom forms part of the domestic economy of the people.

The most shocking thing in China, to a person from the West, is the sight of great numbers of the unburied dead in some of the fields. This is especially the case in the vicinity of Shanghai. Such a state of affairs must be very much against the laws of health. Driving along one of the chief boulevards just out of the city, I noticed scores of coffins of all sizes unburied, and upon inquiry found that there were several reasons for this unusual sight. Many people die whose relatives are too poor to purchase a grave ; in such case no provision is made for burial by the authorities, but the dead are embalmed and the coffin placed in the open field. This is the principal reason for so many remaining uninterred. In other places, large tracts of land have been given for the burial of the dead ; these have become overcrowded, and the coffins have been taken out and set against the mounds and left there. Other tracts in the vicinity could not be given for such purposes, for every foot of productive land in China is utilized in producing rice for the support of the millions. Think of a country so densely populated that there is no room in it to bury their dead !

I was told that cremation was the usual custom of disposing of the dead in some parts of the empire, but in no place did I see it practiced. After seeing the great numbers of unburied, I thought it would be a blessing to China if cremation were adopted as the universal rule. Many regard the process of burning as the highest expression of all heartlessness. We come to have almost a reverence for these shells of ours, made up of perishable matter. A departure from the usual line seems to shock the average person. As we become more enlightened, we shall probably learn that the welfare of the living is an object of greater concern than the final disposition of that portion of ourselves to which we can only attach the same value that we do to a worn-out and useless garment, which, having accomplished its purpose, is cast aside. As we become more enlightened we shall also learn that it is possible to burn our dead with the same reverence and respect as that with which we now consign them to the ravages of the worms of the dust, knowing that in all probability future generations (when the burial-places of to-day are lost to sight) will subsist upon the vegetation nourished by moldering ancestors. Aside from the question of health, cremation would be a perfect boon to that portion of humanity who are so constituted that they must visit the graves of their dear ones in order to express their heart's sorrow. I would just as soon think of weeping over the spot where the cast-off garments of the dead were buried as to go to the cemetery, and in anguish of soul linger beside the spot where the worn-out, cast-off garment of a personality has been buried.

CHAPTER III

HE sights of China prepared me for anything I might see in other parts ; therefore I was not shocked when I reached Siam and learned that the poor of that country, when dead, were thrown to the vultures. A large place in one of the temple grounds is set aside as the spot to which the common dead are brought. In company with a lady I drove to one of these grounds, but on entering a native told us the dead had not yet been brought. Because of the intense heat it is a law that the dead must be disposed of within twenty-four hours ; and as death usually occurs at night the early morning finds every preparation made for the final disposition of the body. We had reached the grounds a little early, but the time was profitably spent in conversation with a most intelligent native, who spoke English very well. He conducted us over the grounds and through the temple, explaining everything of interest. Soon a messenger came to us to say that a Chinese had dropped dead in the gambling-house over the way, and would soon be brought in. On his person money enough was found to pay for the wood, and his remains were to be cremated. As we walked toward the gateway we saw several men carrying a rough pine

box covered with a red blanket; this was placed to
one side in a sheltered spot, and the men began preparations for cremation. From one corner of the ground
they brought quantities of wood, split in the usual
length for a stove; a high, long pile was arranged,
and before the box was removed to the pile, the natives asked if we cared to see the dead Chinaman.
We walked over to the box, the red blanket was removed, and we saw that the friendless man had been
packed away with his few effects, all of which were to
be consigned to the fire. The cover was replaced,
and box, blanket and all were lifted upon the pile.
A match was touched to the wood, the pyre was
wrapped in clouds of smoke, and long tongues of
flame soon reduced all to a small pile of ashes.

Meantime some of the dead Siamese had been
brought in, having been carried through the streets
in an entirely nude condition on a rough plank borne
on the shoulders of the natives. To prevent the remains from falling into the street, runners had kept
beside the plank to replace a limb or arm upon the
board as it was jolted from its resting-place by the
motion of the bearers. Beside the spot reserved for
burning the dead was a small square, fenced off by
a solid brick wall some four feet high. Within this
a still smaller space was marked off by a row of
bricks, and in the second inclosure the dead were
disposed of. Perched on the fence and on the eaves
of the temple sat a row of solemn-faced vultures,
waiting for their prey. The bearers advanced to the
gate and tossed the remains into the little square.

In an instant every vulture had scented the dead and swooped down to the spot. In thirty-five minutes every bone was picked bare and no trace of flesh remained.

Only the lower classes and criminals are disposed of in this way. Special arrangements are made for the cremation of the dead of the royal household. The ceremony is more like some festive occasion than one of sadness. Large buildings are erected at great cost, and all the people are given up wholly to the ceremonies. When the body has been reduced to ashes, a golden vase, in the form of the king's decoration on his umbrella, is brought in and the sacred dust deposited in the vessel, which is placed in one of the rooms of the palace beside other vases containing similar relics of the dead. The buildings are then torn down, and the imperial family put on mourning and make the usual display of grief.

In the vast country of India the dead are disposed of according to the religious belief that prevails in different parts of the country. The Brahmins burn their dead in public places. (This custom I have referred to on pages 231–233). The Mohammedans bury them and place a heavy, flat stone over the grave. And the Parsees, the most intelligent of all the people of Asia, and, I should say, the most highly educated, build great towers, within which the dead are placed, to be devoured by the ever-present vulture.

The Parsees, who came over from Persia some few centuries ago, have settled in great numbers in the

Bombay presidency. In their energy in carrying on commercial pursuits they outdo, if anything, the Hebrew. Their steady application to business has made them the leaders of trade in that presidency. Settling there in early days, they brought with them the peculiar custom of disposing of their dead that had been handed down to them through all the centuries, and probably will be practiced through the coming ages.

One of the most beautiful spots along the coast, without the city of Bombay, is the site of the Parsee "Towers of Silence." A very high stone wall surrounds the entire grounds, which include some acres; the whole is laid out like a beautiful and extensive park, and well in toward the center stand the three towers. Just why they are called towers would be hard to say, for they are more like unroofed round houses. They are about forty-five feet high, and perhaps the same in diameter, built of brick and plastered over with gray cement. Near the top, at one side, are two iron doors, which are always locked when there is not a funeral taking place. About ten feet from the top, on the inside, fastened to the wall a few feet apart, and extending in a slight incline toward the center, is an iron grating, upon which the remains are placed. The bars meet within two feet at the center. Each iron bar is curved toward the center, forming a small channel, down which all moisture from the body is carried. The bottom is very deep and extends some hundreds of feet into the earth. The oldest tower has been in use for two hundred and fifty years. These grounds are the home of the vultures, and at any time

of the day and night they can be seen in numbers
perched upon the top of the towers and along the
edge of the fence. They stand perfectly motionless,
and as they are huddled one against the other it is
easy to mistake them for the parapet of the towers.
Their long, gray plumage, well dressed and trimmed,
has almost the effect of polished stone, and for a moment I mistook them for an ornamental finish to the
structures.

By securing a pass from the authorities the grounds
may be visited at stated hours. The funerals take
place at given times, and no foreigner is then allowed
in the grounds ; even the Parsee women are excluded
from attendance. One day, when the heat was almost
past endurance, I was invited to drive out and view
the place. Nothing but my great desire to fully
understand the Parsee burial customs would have
tempted me from the house, but such is human thirst
after knowledge (to say nothing of curiosity) that
even the scorching glare of old Sol became a matter
of little moment. Casting aside every garment that
could well be disposed of, I borrowed a gentleman's
cork hat to prevent sunstroke, or, as they say in that
country, "a touch of the sun," and started along the
beach in the direction of the "Towers of Silence."
Ascending the steps we were confronted by a sign
printed in the English language, which warned us not
to be found on the grounds after a certain hour. In
response to a ring of the bell, the porter opened the
gate ; our passes were examined, and we walked into
the corridor, where a miniature tower was explained

by this chatty individual. We passed into the
grounds, and the little Parsee lady who accompanied
me fairly gasped for breath as I hurled handfuls of
interrogation-points at her, and wrote down her cheerful information in my note-book. The time passed
faster than I had thought ; indeed I was so interested
in this little woman's explanation that I took no note
of time, and when the funeral hour came around we
found that we were locked in the grounds. The ring-
ing of the bell and a knock at the gate reminded
me that a funeral procession was about to enter. I
did not know what the penalty might be for this
intrusion, which on my part was quite unintentional,
but I resolved to " stand ground " and face it out.
My friend suggested that we quietly retreat, and seek
the entrance by a less frequented path, but " retreat "
does not figure largely in my make-up. I hastily
settled in my own mind a plan of action. From long
association with all ranks and conditions of men, I
have learned that a good way of escape out of a difficulty is to smile one's way through. I stepped
toward the porter with as much of a smile as the
solemnity of the occasion warranted, and in penitent
tones expressed my deep regret at having transgressed
the law, but suggested that, as I was already in forbidden grounds, it would be much better to remain ;
and, placing a coin in his hand, I seated myself where
I could command a full view of the procession.

Those who attended the funeral drove up in carriages, but the remains were brought through the
streets on a bamboo litter, the poles resting on the

shoulders of two front and rear bearers, and the sides
on those of four marching between the front and rear
men. As they reached the steps, the bearers of the
dead headed the procession. They wore long, white
dresses that fell from their neck to the ground, and
were girded at the waist with a sash of the same
material. The fingers of each hand were bound
about with white gauze, and a mitten of the same
goods was pulled over the hands. This was to prevent any possible contact with the unclothed dead, for
the remains were only covered with a sheet. The
relatives and mourners, some ten in all, followed two
abreast, without demonstration of any kind ; a coolie
brought up the rear, leading a little yellow dog by a
string. This strange procession moved slowly toward
the tower. The iron doors on the side had been
opened and a ladder placed before it. Up this the
priest made his way, and the remains were handed to
him, that he might place them upon the grating ; this
done, the little yellow dog, which protested loudly,
was also handed up and placed in the tower for a few
moments. The sheet was removed, the dog handed
down, the descent of the priest was accomplished, the
pall-bearers drew from their fingers the wrappings,
and the iron doors were shut. At this particular
time there chanced to be no vultures on that tower,
but they had settled in numbers on the others near
by. During the entire ceremony they " perched and
sat, nothing more," not even a feather moving ; but
the moment they heard the click of the iron door it
served as a signal to call them to action. They rose,

as if on one wing, and settled in the interior of the tower. We remained seated for about half an hour, and saw the birds return to their perch, knowing that every atom of flesh had been devoured, and the bones had fallen from the grating to the bottom, some two hundred feet below.

When the dog is placed in the tower with the remains, his movements are watched by the priest. Should he go over and kiss the face of the dead, it signifies a happy and eternal repose ; but failing to do this, the news is reported to the family of the departed one, and his name is never again spoken within the household.

THE END.

www.ingramcontent.com/pod-product-compliance
Lightning Source LLC
Chambersburg PA
CBHW060519030726

47498CB00004B/1006